Tom couldn't explain what happened next.

Something about Wednesday's warm laughter, her sparkling eyes, or her heavenly lavender scent—something he couldn't quite define—captivated him.

His hands gripped her firmly at the hips, pulling her close. Wednesday didn't struggle. Instead, she stopped laughing, and Tom saw the twinkling light in her eyes vanish, replaced with something else, something heated—glowing and vibrant with need. Hot, steaming, scorching desire churned in his belly.

The feel of her hips under his hands drove him mad. He took a deep breath, laced his fingers in the loops of her jeans, and enjoyed the sensation of having her body close to his.

He should back away. He drew her nearer. She came willingly. He shouldn't kiss her. He was her employer. They didn't have a future together. But how could he resist her? She was so deliciously charming, and she had a great set of lips he wanted to taste. He couldn't wait to feel those lips against his.

"Wednesday," he murmured, gazing down into her upturned face.

"Dr. Anderson," she murmured back.

"Tom," he corrected.

"Tom," she whispered.

"I'm going to kiss you." His hands spanned her waist.

She nodded, giving a small gasp as he pulled her tight against him, lowering his lips to hers.

Wednesday melted like soft caramel against him, her arms reaching up across his shoulders, encircling his neck. His lips slowly played across hers, sweet, warm, and enticing. She responded beneath his touch, her lips hungrily opening against his. Wave after wave of desire flowed through his body, and he didn't want it to stop.

Dr. Anderson's Nanny

by

Amy Hahn

This is a work of fiction. Names, characters, places, and incidents either are the product of the author's imagination or are used fictitiously, and any resemblance to actual persons living or dead, business establishments, events, or locales, is entirely coincidental.

Dr. Anderson's Nanny

Contact Information: info@thewildrosepress.com

Cover Art by *Tamra Westberry*

The Wild Rose Press
PO Box 708
Adams Basin, NY 14410-0706
Visit us at www.thewildrosepress.com

Publishing History
First Faery Rose Edition, 2009
Print ISBN 1-60154-690-4

Published in the United States of America

Dedication

To my two fabulous sisters, Jessica and Emily.
There is magic in each of you.

Prologue

Lumina, a fairy employed by the "Magical Nannies for Children Foundation," watched seven-year-old Jenna Anderson struggle to write an ad for a nanny.

Jenna had been sitting at the little writing desk near the fireplace for more than an hour. Her legs dangled over the edge of her chair, her small feet barely brushing the polished wood floor.

Lumina's heart went out to the young girl struggling to make the words just right. She was having problems putting her needs into words, after all, how does one ask for the perfect nanny?

"What I really want is Mary Poppins," Jenna said softly, "but not everyone can be as lucky as Jane and Michael Banks." She chewed on the edge of a pink pencil, a crease lining the smooth skin of her forehead.

Lumina smiled. That was most certainly true. Jane and Michael Banks had been very lucky, but nannies like Mary Poppins did exist, and it was Lumina's job to match up the magical nannies with children who needed them.

She knew Jenna's father, Dr. Tom Anderson had placed his own ad in the local paper, but she didn't like it one bit. He asked for someone who sounded absolutely normal, when all the time, Lumina knew his three daughters needed someone special, far more special than he could ever imagine.

Jenna sighed and dropped the pencil on the table. Tears filled her big blue eyes. She quickly brushed them away with the back of her hand.

"Mommy." The child's sad little voice caused Lumina's throat to tighten.

Lumina hugged her knees to her chest, and the tips of her bare toes curled around the edge of the fireplace mantle.

Jenna reached for the photo in front of her. Her fingers trembled against the silvery frame. Lumina knew it was a picture of Jenna's mother, Mary, who'd died in a car accident two years ago. Lumina had been studying the Andersons for the last two weeks. Part of her job was observing the family before giving her recommendations to the Foundation and selecting the perfect nanny to help the family heal.

"I miss you." Jenna's girlish voice was at a whisper volume so her father, who was reading in the next room, didn't hear her.

Lumina studied the photo from her perch on the mantle. The woman was lovely, blonde and blue-eyed with a vibrant smile. The image of Mary radiated warmth, love, and joy of life. From her research, it sounded as if Mary had been a wonderful mother, friend, wife and daughter, as well as a community activist.

Jenna traced the lines of her mother's lovely face. Lumina knew Jenna sometimes fell asleep talking to her mother, missing her and needing her. There was a terrible longing deep inside the little girl. It was understandable and so very sad. Mortal life was so unfair. It was so fleeting and filled with such sadness. But it was also overflowing with unbelievable happiness, ordinary mortal magic more powerful than that conjured by magical creatures such as herself.

Lumina sniffed, wiping her nose with a lacy handkerchief.

"Jenna, are you finished with your letter?" called Tom Anderson from the nearby library.

Jenna looked away from her mother's face. She brushed away more tears from her cheeks and answered with forced cheerfulness, "Almost."

"Good. It's time for bed. Ten more minutes."

Jenna glanced toward the doorway leading to her father's favorite room. Lumina could see only Dr. Anderson's legs and his stocking feet; he wore bright red socks. He sat in a large leather chair with his back to her. The huge chair swallowed him in its comfy depths.

Jenna picked up the pencil again and stared at the blank sheet of paper in front of her. Lumina wanted to help, but that sort of help was forbidden. She was not allowed to interact with possible charges. That was the responsibility of the nanny selected for the position.

The little girl quickly scribbled some words down in her scrawling print and sighed as she gazed at the wobbly letters. Fresh tears streamed down her cheeks. She slammed her pencil down. Lumina jumped soundlessly to her feet.

The noise caused Dr. Anderson to lean forward in his chair and look in Jenna's direction. "Jenna, is there something wrong?" he asked gently.

"No, nothing's wrong." Jenna leaned as far back in her chair as she could, trying to hide from her father's line of vision and brushed the tears away from her cheeks.

The poor thing. She never let her father see her cry. She tried to be her father's rock. She was a strong little thing. Her mother's death had made her much older than her seven years. Lumina knew she took being the eldest very seriously. Jenna felt it was up to her to look after her father and two sisters, five-year-old Tamra and three-year-old Michaela.

"Are you finished with your project?" Tom asked.

Jenna crumpled up the piece of white notebook

paper and tossed it on the floor. She'd given up. Lumina's heart tightened.

Lumina watched as Tom Anderson closed the medical journal and placed it on the top of the very large mahogany desk. He stood up, turned off the light, and walked into the living room where Jenna sat staring forlornly at a crumpled piece of white paper.

"Jenna, baby, let's go to bed," he said, offering his daughter a warm smile.

Lumina's heart warmed. He really was a kind, caring father, and one who dearly loved his children. But he distanced himself as much as possible, throwing himself into his work, hiring nanny after nanny after nanny to fulfill both mother and father roles for his children.

Jenna glanced up and returned his smile. She jumped off the chair and walked toward him in her pink-footed pajamas. Tom leaned down and wrapped Jenna in his arms, holding her close against his broad chest as he kissed the top of her head. She wrapped small arms about his neck and buried her face in the folds of his white polo shirt. She closed her tired eyes and sighed as he lifted her, cradling her gently.

"What were you writing?" he asked softly.

"I wrote nothing," she told him, looking up at into his concerned face.

"A little writer's block?" he asked, heading for the stairs.

Lumina fluttered soundlessly to the floor, snatching up the discarded piece of paper. It was almost as big as she was, but with a little magic it shrank significantly enough for her to fold it neatly and place it in a small pocket of her green dress. She rose off the floor, following behind the father and daughter at a safe distance. She didn't want them to see her. Her job was to stay invisible.

Jenna nodded tiredly and snuggled close against her father. She looked so happy in her father's arms. Lumina hugged herself tightly as she flew behind them, knowing the precious child enjoyed the few moments she had with Tom. He would be busy at work tomorrow. Long shifts as a pediatric cardiac surgeon kept him away all too often.

Lumina hid behind the doorframe, watching as Tom tucked Jenna into bed. He gave her a loving kiss, and flipped off the bedroom light. "Goodnight, baby."

"Goodnight, Daddy." Jenna's eyes closed as she curled on her side, the fist of a small hand pressed against one rosy cheek.

Tom watched his daughter for a few moments before slipping out of the room and back down the stairs.

"Don't worry, little one," Lumina whispered, blowing Jenna a kiss, "all will be well. I promise."

Jenna smiled and turned onto her other side, facing away from Lumina.

Lumina followed Tom into the living room, flying over to the mantle to hide behind the old-fashioned clock that was its centerpiece. Tom walked to where the piece of paper had been, frowning as he looked around and underneath the desk. He scratched his head, clearly puzzled. He expanded his search until he'd walked around the entire room.

"Now that's odd," he said quietly, gazing about the room.

The clock chimed ten o'clock, startling Lumina so much she almost lost her balance. She covered her ears with her hands. It was horribly loud, at least to her. But to Tom, it was nothing out of the ordinary. The quiet hum of music from an antique radio in the corner also filled the room. The house creaked and groaned its familiar sounds.

Tom shrugged and went into the kitchen. She

suspected he'd go through the process of making his ritual evening snack.

Lumina watched him leave the room before she bounced off the mantle and promptly flew up the chimney, iridescent wings fluttering quietly in the night. She flew through the evening sky, moving up, up toward the glimmering stars.

Her observation was over, and her assignment completed. She'd found children who needed a magical nanny, and they needed one desperately.

Lumina had just the right someone in mind.

Chapter One

Wednesday stood outside the front door of Dr. Thomas Anderson's two-story Victorian. The sweeping front porch practically surrounded the entire house. Mixed amid an array of vibrant red and yellow roses stood tall oaks and maple trees. The grass in front of the house was nothing if not the perfectly manicured lawn, green as a St. Patrick's Day four-leaf clover. Not a single dandelion dared splatter the solid emerald carpet with its presence. A high brick wall, covered in ivy and honeysuckle, lined the perimeter of the entire property.

She smoothed slips of hair away from her face. She was the perfect nanny for his children, but he didn't know it yet. She'd have to convince him of that first and it might not be easy. "I hope he likes me," Wednesday whispered. "If he doesn't, I might have to resort to a little bit of magic."

Nervous butterflies fluttered in her stomach. She really wanted this job. This job would prove to the "Magical Nannies for Children Foundation" she was a spectacular magical nanny. She couldn't afford to make mistakes since her very career as a nanny depended on this one job.

She reached forward and rang the doorbell, cocking her head to one side as she listened to it chime through the big house. Soon she heard the heavy footsteps of a man approach. She backed away from the door and waited for Dr. Thomas Anderson to appear. The door opened and in front of her stood the father of the distressed child who had written the letter Wednesday kept folded inside her purse.

She'd read it so many times that it was torn at the edges with a few tear-smeared words and salty watermarks. She knew him from the picture Lumina had shown her.

She impulsively took another step back to gaze up at the tall man before her. Gray peppered his midnight hair and he practically filled the entire doorway with his muscular bulk. He stood at least six feet tall, dressed in jeans that hugged his hips and legs in a sexy loose style. A white T-shirt pulled attractively across his well-toned pectorals and biceps. The man was tan, very tan, and his eyes were a dark, mesmerizing green.

Dr. Anderson was much more handsome than his photo. Lumina had forgotten to mention that fact. Of course, she'd been more focused on learning about Jenna, Tamra and Michaela than on him at the time.

Still, Lumina should've warned her. Wednesday made a mental note to strangle the fairy the next time she saw her.

And he smelled good. Fresh and clean. Soapy. And he didn't look at all happy to see her.

Wednesday swallowed hard and reached out a trembling hand.

"Hello," she said, keeping her voice strong and steady, even though her insides had turned to mush. She was so nervous. And it wasn't only because her career depended on this job, her jitters had to do with the fact the man standing before her was incredibly delicious looking.

Yep, that would be the main reason.

"Who are you?" Dr. Thomas Anderson leaned against the doorframe and studied her with his dark green eyes.

Wednesday gulped. She forced herself from taking another step back. She was behaving like a ninny. She'd absolutely nothing to be afraid of. After all, she was a witch. She could turn him into a toad if he made her too angry.

"I'm here about the nanny position."

He raised one eyebrow, his eyes glowing with amusement. Wednesday knew that look meant he clearly didn't think she was nanny material. "Really?" he said.

"I can assure you, I'm a nanny, and a very good one," Wednesday proclaimed with far more confidence than she felt. "I have references."

That was a lie. She hated to lie, but she wanted this job. She was the perfect candidate, hand chosen by Lumina who was an expert in placing magical nannies in mortal and magical homes. She should have thought to conjure a list of references up earlier, but she hadn't actually thought that far ahead. She'd been far too excited.

He examined her, looking her up and down, and turned away. "I don't believe you're what I had in mind," he replied softly.

"What or whom *did* you have in mind?" she inquired curiously.

"Someone more mature..." he looked her up and down and corrected himself "...grandmotherly."

"I can be nurturing, motherly, if that's what's bothering you," she tossed at him.

His look clearly said he didn't believe her.

She took a deep breath and boldly moved past him as she let herself into the spacious foyer, walking around him. "I'm older than you think." She was willing to shove him aside, if need be, to make her point.

"Hey," he exclaimed, "Just what do you think you're doing?"

She spun around and held out her hand. "Should we try this again?"

He stared at her in astonishment. "I don't think so."

"Why not?" She pulled her hand back and smiled. "I believe your nanny position is now filled."

He gaped at her. "What? I haven't hired you."

She looked him straight in the eye. "You haven't hired me, Dr. Anderson. Your children have."

His look of flabbergasted amazement amused her. Wednesday figured he was moments away from calling the police. It was obvious he thought she was out of her mind. A normal person wouldn't just invite herself in and make such a statement. She had to do something to convince him she wasn't crazy.

"I think I heard you wrong." He walked away from the door toward her.

"No. You heard me correctly, Dr. Anderson."

"I'm not about to hire a person I haven't even interviewed to watch my children. Not only haven't I interviewed you, I haven't even asked you to interview for the job." He jutted his thumb at the door behind him. "Please leave, I'm expecting someone."

"I completely understand your point," she said. "Why don't you interview me so you'll feel better? I suggest we start now."

Wednesday wasn't going anywhere until he agreed to hire her. The children needed her. She wasn't about to let them down. Lumina's report had broken her heart.

He shook his head. She went right on talking, "Then, you can find out more about me."

He continued shaking his head. "I have appointments all day for the nanny position. The first one is in less than an hour and all the applicants are from respectable agencies," he said. "And who *are* you, anyway? I doubt you're my first interviewee. Is your name Beatrice?"

She blushed. "I apologize. I was so excited about this position, I forgot to tell you my name." She smiled, stepping forward and holding out her hand again. "My name is Wednesday."

She stood inches away from him. She was almost tall enough to look him in the eye, but not quite. Her chin slanted up at a slight angle, just a tiny bit when she met his gaze. Her forehead leveled with the tip of his nose and she tilted back her head to get a better look at him.

"Wednesday?" One eyebrow jutted up in a thick arch. "That's an odd name."

"It is not," she said in defense. Mortals could be really rude. They really did need to be more open-minded. She placed her hands on her hips.

"You just don't run into a lot of people with that name," he said. "The only person who comes to mind…"

He paused and she wondered why he didn't finish.

"Who? Go ahead," she encouraged.

"Wednesday Addams is the only character I've heard called Wednesday—the television character from the Addams Family."

She said nothing for a moment. What could she say? Instead she sighed with exasperation. "I know people think my name is odd. Very few people name their children after days of the week. I guess you could say I'm unique."

He had no idea just how very unique.

"I apologize for teasing you about your name. I didn't mean to insult you." He cleared his throat and tried again. "What is your last name?"

"What?" she squeaked, startled by his question.

She wasn't used to supplying a last name. Why hadn't Lumina reminded her? It had been awhile since she'd walked amongst mortals, other than her very mortal brother-in-law. She'd forgotten they all had last names. Witches did not. She was simply Wednesday, daughter of Sunday. Lumina should've warned her about that as well.

"Your last name? You do have a last name?" he asked.

No. She did not. But she couldn't tell him that. "Hmmm, last name?"

"Yes, a last name," said Tom, eyeing her as if she'd just announced she was from Venus. "Everyone has a last name."

"Wednesday…Wednesday." She flashed what she hoped was a bewitchingly brilliant smile.

Tom Anderson's laughter filled the room, a charming, deep, rich and infectious rumble.

"You can't be serious."

"I most certainly am." She stuck out her chin and flashed him her most charming smile.

"I don't think so," Tom said. His laughter faded. "However, I do appreciate your humor."

"Okay, then, Wednesday…Green."

"You sound hesitant, as if you're making up the name. Are you sure about that?"

She nodded. "Absolutely." She doubted he'd appreciate knowing she'd made the last name up after looking into his eyes. No, she couldn't tell him that, although green was fast becoming her favorite color.

"I'm very glad to meet you, Miss Wednesday Green." He reached out and took her hand.

The soft warmth of his touch startled her. The sensation of his skin against hers thrilled her. She fought the strange urge to lean forward and kiss him. The feeling was overwhelming. His fingers slid with enticing slowness along hers. His hand lingered a bit too long to be proper. The touch on hers was so soft her sensitive fingertips tingled. Wednesday, realizing she enjoyed the touch far too much, withdrew her hand completely.

He walked over to the long hall table lining one wall of the spacious foyer, picked up a pen and clipboard, and glanced down at the sheet of paper. He slipped on his reading glasses.

Wednesday thought he looked adorably handsome wearing his glasses.

"You aren't on my list, Miss Green. I have a Miss Beatrice Granger at noon and a Miss Marnie Walsh at one and a Miss Naomi Williams at two and a Miss Clara Statler at three." He stopped and turned back to ask her, "What agency did you say you work for?"

"I don't work for an agency. Remember? I work for myself."

"Well, whether you work for an agency or for yourself doesn't matter much." Tom's black-rimmed glasses slid slightly down his nose, and he gazed at her over the tops of his spectacles. "What matters to me most is if you are a good caretaker for my children and have good references."

"I can assure you, I'm a very good nanny with excellent references." Her voice choked on the fib. She may not have a list of references with her, but she could whip up a list in a flash if necessary.

"Good." Tom set down the clipboard and walked back to her.

Wednesday beamed. It looked like she might have won this man over, but his next words caused the smile to vanish from her lips.

"May I please see them?" he asked, reaching out a hand.

The strap of her oversized handbag slipped down her arm. She pushed it back into place. "See what?"

"Your references. You did bring them, didn't you?"

"Of course!" She groaned internally. She hated to lie, especially to the father of her future charges.

"Are you going to show them to me or not?" he asked, folding his arms across his chest.

Wednesday placed one hand in her bag. It was a straw bag with bright pink and blue flowers. It looked more like it belonged on a beach in California than in ocean-less Minnesota. Of course, the state was not named Land of 10,000 Lakes for nothing. She closed her eyes briefly and conjured up a resume and list of references. Her fingers curled about the edge of the smooth paper.

"Here it is," she said triumphantly, pulling the paper out of the straw bag with a flourish and handing it to him.

Tom took the page of linen résumé paper, adjusted his glasses, and briefly skimmed the five names listed, all neatly typed.

"Is that sufficient?" she asked, leaning forward. "I can provide more if you need them."

"No, five should be enough."

"Great!" she exclaimed. This interview process was going much better than she'd expected at first.

He took a step away from her and cleared his throat. "You'll have to come back tomorrow. I'm interviewing more nannies then."

Wednesday noticed he avoided looking directly into her eyes. She'd affected him. He'd affected her as well. It wasn't good to be this attracted to her future employer. She pushed the thought from her mind, refusing to worry about it.

"Can't you interview me now? After all, I'm here."

"I'm a busy man. I live and work by appointments, Miss Green," Tom said gruffly. He placed the résumé and list of references on the hallway table next to the clipboard. "I have Miss Granger in twenty minutes, and that wouldn't be enough time to sufficiently interview you. I'm quite particular when it comes to the care of my children."

He'd already made that point perfectly clear. His concern and dedication for their welfare said much about his love for the three little girls. He was a good man and father. He just needed a little help to guide him back to spending more time with his adorable daughters. The children needed more time with their father. A nanny could never take the place of a parent.

And Wednesday knew she was the witch to accomplish that difficult task.

"I understand," she said. "What time tomorrow?"

He picked up the clipboard and glanced at it. "How about four in the afternoon? I have a slot open then."

"Fine." She tried to keep the disappointment from showing in her voice, which was a very hard thing to accomplish. She was sure it showed since she'd always found it difficult to hide her feelings. "That'll be just fine. I'll be here promptly at four."

He added her name to the list. "I must say you have a strange way of going about interviewing, Miss Green. Most people call first to inquire about the job before showing up or wait to be called and invited."

"I'm not like most people. I prefer the direct approach." She adjusted the strap of the straw purse as it slid, once again off her shoulder and down her arm.

He grinned. Her insides melted. He possessed the most attractive grin. She casually looked him over. There had to be something she didn't like about him.

"No, you are not like most people," he agreed. "However, in my ad I stated all those interested should call me to set up an interview time."

"Oh, I'm sorry, but I never saw *your* ad, Dr. Anderson." She smoothed a loose curl away from her cheek. Good gracious, hadn't he heard her the first time?

He leaned back against the wall and removed

the reading glasses, folding the bows of the spectacles with one hand and resting the piece of optometry against the crook of his elbow as he crossed his arms in front of his chest.

"If you don't work for an agency—I contacted three—and you didn't answer my ad in the paper, how did you learn about the job?" he asked, tilting his head to one side as he watched her.

Wednesday forced herself to smile and said cheerfully, "I told you before. I answered your children's ad for a nanny—actually, an ad written by one of your children. I didn't answer yours."

His eyebrows arched. Suspicion darkened his eyes. "Explain. My children didn't write an ad."

Wednesday gulped nervously. She realized, too late, she'd shared too much. Once again, she'd spoken before thinking. It was a habit of hers and not necessarily a good one. She shifted anxiously from one foot to the other, once again tugging at the strap of her bag as it slid off her slim shoulder. Now she had to come up with an explanation for what she'd just blurted out. A respectable surgeon such as Dr. Anderson wouldn't understand. He'd toss her in a loony bin quicker than she could say dynamite, which is exactly what she thought about their interactions. He was dynamite and she was going to explode. Or, maybe it was the other way around.

She wished he'd forget she'd said anything about Jenna's ad. She moved her hand slowly in front of his face and magicked his thoughts away. It really was the best way to deal with the awkward situation. Although, she really should try to learn to deal with mortals without the use of magic. She needed to work on that.

Tom blinked as her hand moved. "What was I saying?" he asked after a few moments of silence.

Wednesday smiled, dropping her hand to her side. "You said I should meet you at four tomorrow afternoon for a formal interview."

"Right." He blinked again, confusion in his eyes. His fingers clutched his glasses so hard Wednesday thought the piece of glassware might bust. "Tomorrow at four."

"Tomorrow at four," Wednesday repeated. "Do I get to meet the children tomorrow?"

Tom shook his head. "No. The children will be at their grandmother's tomorrow."

"Don't you think the children should meet prospective nannies?" she asked sweetly, instantly regretting her remark when she received a full blast of frigid cold from eyes. She held her hands in front of her, palms facing him. "Perhaps I overstepped by bounds with that question"

Tom didn't say a word. She saw the doubt flickering in the emerald pools of his eyes and her heart jumped nervously. She didn't want to lose this job and she couldn't possibly wait until tomorrow for an interview.

Suddenly, she had an amazing, wonderful, perfectly magical idea.

"Perhaps someone will cancel today, and you'll be able to interview me," she said brightly.

"I doubt it." He gestured to the open front door. "Let me show you out."

"Oh, I can show myself out." She slipped past him, walking slowly towards the door.

She would have to use a little more magic to hurry this interview process along. She certainly didn't need any competition.

The phone rang right on cue. She smiled, stopping at the front door. She turned to watch Tom answer. She noticed dozens of pictures lined the long foyer table, photos of his smiling, adorable daughters and of his deceased wife. She knew all about Mary and the girls. Lumina's report on Case #1168 had thoroughly informed her about the Anderson situation.

Tom watched her. She stared back and offered him a friendly smile. “Hello,” he said into the phone. “Oh, hello, Miss Granger.”

Wednesday flipped a strand of dark hair across one shoulder, the shoulder without the slipping purse strap. She leaned against the doorframe, trying to look innocent and uninterested in the present phone conversation. She looked away from him and pretended to study the tip of her bare big toe, speculating about the polish color. She thought ‘Planted in Spring Pink’ was the perfect choice. But even while she admired the bright pink enamel, her attention never wavered from the phone conversation. She knew exactly what was about to happen. She’d planned it.

“Oh, well, that’s too bad. I was looking forward to talking with you. Are you ill?”

Wednesday looked up and smiled.

There was a long pause before she heard him murmur softly, “Congratulations on the new job.” Another pause and then, “I’m sure I’ll find a perfectly wonderful person to take care of my children. Thank you, Miss Granger.” He set the receiver back in its cradle.

Wednesday tried to act as if she’d been staring at the photos on the hallway table and not listening to the conversation. She readjusted her purse strap, thinking she should do something to fix the darn thing. She needed to keep it form constantly slipping. “I’ll see you tomorrow, Dr. Anderson. Have a good day.”

Tom looked at her incredulously. “It seems Miss Granger has accepted another job and can’t make it today.”

“What a shame!” exclaimed Wednesday, feigning dismay. She took a step over the threshold. “I’ll see you tomorrow.”

"Wait." He closed the distance between them in three strides. "It seems I have some time now. Would you like your interview now?"

Wednesday's heart soared. She stepped back into the foyer...and promptly tripped on a discarded stuffed animal. She tumbled forward with a small cry.

How had she missed that?

He caught her. Wednesday felt his lips brush her forehead and the curve of her ear as she fell into the warm strength of his arms. He jerked his face away from hers. Her skin tingled from his intimate touch. His body was all delicious masculine hardness against hers.

"Thank you," Wednesday whispered as he helped her regain her balance. They stood close together. His hands lingered lightly against the small of her back.

She knew her face flamed red. His touch left hot impressions wherever they made contact. Her ears were ultra sensitive, her most erotic spot. She still felt the branding heat of his lips on the tender skin of her ear.

She was such a klutz sometimes. "I hope you don't hire people based on how graceful they are."

He laughed, removing his hands from the small of her back. "Don't worry, that isn't one of the criteria I look for."

Wednesday sighed with relief, laughing nervously.

He was too close. She smelled the clean delicious scent of him. Her knees went weak, forcing her to place more weight against his tall frame.

"I'd love to interview now," she said.

She gazed up at him and knew instinctively she should ask Lumina to find someone else for the position. She liked him too much. The feelings he evoked might distract her from what she needed to do. Her focus had to be on healing the relationship between Tom and his daughters. Romance was not on the agenda. And yet, she couldn't help but remember the feel of his skin against hers, the brush of his lips along the curve of her ear.

She shivered. Her heart skipped a beat.

This scenario had disaster written all over it.

Chapter Two

When all the other nannies backed out on him, Tom had no other choice but to ask Wednesday Green back. He scheduled her for a second interview two days later, an interview with his children.

He simply had no other prospects.

Two of the possible nannies said they were sick, three others said they accepted other jobs, and the final person, a Miss Trinny, decided to make a drastic career change, from child provider to nun. Tom could only shake his head in disbelief after each phone call. He had the eerie feeling the famed Fates from Greek legends worked overtime against him.

The interview lasted the whole afternoon and into the evening. The children quizzed Wednesday on absolutely everything. They asked her about her favorite pet and if she preferred chocolate chip cookies to sugar cookies. They wanted to know if she would read to them. They hoped she liked peanut butter sandwiches with sliced bananas on top. Tamra wanted to know if she liked horses. Michaela asked if she watched Disney movies. Jenna asked if she enjoyed the park.

Tom sat silent through most of the questions, thoroughly amused as he watched his children interrogate Wednesday. He admired how she took it all in stride, a warm smile lifting the corners of her mouth, her eyes sparkling. She gave the children her complete attention.

He didn't doubt she loved children. She seemed genuinely interested in their questions, interests, and opinions. It soon became evident to him his girls adored her. He'd have a difficult time denying them their choice in a nanny, and yet he felt he couldn't possibly hire her. He needed an older, wiser, and less attractive nanny than Wednesday Green, preferably a grandma with graying hair and spectacles and too many wrinkles to count.

Wednesday answered each and every one of their questions with a patience that amazed Tom. Her favorite pet was a cat, although she loved all animals. She liked chocolate chip cookies best. She simply adored books and would read to them every day. She definitely knew how to make peanut butter sandwiches with sliced bananas, but only if the girls shared, because those sandwiches were her ultimate favorite food. And, yes, she did love Disney movies, knew how to ride horses, and found long walks in the park absolutely delightful.

After a few hours, Tom glanced at his watch. He shook his head in amazement. He couldn't believe his children interviewed Wednesday for so long. The entire day faded away quickly. He hadn't even noticed when the rays of the warm sun started to disappear into the west. He was far too busy staring at Miss Wednesday Green who captivated his as much as she did his children.

"Don't you think we should wrap this up?" he finally asked Jenna. He glanced back at his watch for emphasis. "It's getting late."

Jenna glowed with happiness. Tom groaned inwardly. It was obvious his eldest didn't want Wednesday to leave. His daughter thought she'd found her version of Mary Poppins, minus the magic of course.

Tom glanced over at Wednesday. They shared a smile. She looked perfectly content on the patio visiting with the three little girls, watching them smile and laugh and act as sisters do. She looked as if she belonged there. The very thought made Tom nervous.

"One more question," Jenna declared with authority, definitely showing she was the boss of the three.

Wednesday placed her elbows on the patio table and leaned forward, giving Jenna her full attention. "Yes?" she asked.

Jenna moved closer. Tom had noticed how she'd inched closer and closer to Wednesday as the afternoon wore on.

"Do you have a boyfriend?" Jenna asked softly, her blue eyes gazing up at Wednesday.

Wednesday flushed attractively. Tom leaned forward, curious to know her answer. He didn't want her to have a boyfriend. But he shouldn't care. He wasn't interested in Wednesday. Or was he? He noticed how she avoided looking at him.

"Not right now."

Jenna smiled widely, obviously satisfied with Wednesday's confession. "Good! That way, we don't have to share you with anyone."

"That is a personal question," Tom interjected. "You aren't allowed to ask that in job interviews."

Jenna didn't even look over at him. He noticed Wednesday bit her lip to keep from laughing. Jenna wasn't only bossy, but had a mind of her own.

"I simply wanted to know if we would have to share her," Jenna said, her voice far more adult than her age.

Tom fought to keep from smiling. Jenna never failed to make him smile. "Well, it's not an appropriate question."

"Well, I can't take it back!" Jenna exclaimed in exasperation. She rolled her eyes.

Mirth lit Wednesday's brown-green eyes. "I don't mind." She looked away from Jenna, her gaze meeting Tom's over Jenna's golden head. "I honestly don't mind."

"I think it's time Miss Green went home," Tom said, looking away from Wednesday and standing. He picked up Michaela who was curled in a chair, almost asleep. "We can talk to her again tomorrow."

"Does she have to go?" whined Jenna, jumping off her chair. "I like having her here.

"Yes. For now. Let's walk her out, shall we?"

"Okay," sighed Jenna. She reached for Wednesday's hand. "Will you hold my hand?"

"Of course I will."

Something warm and tender curled its way about Tom's heart as he watched Wednesday take his daughter's small hand in hers. He was astonished to feel moisture in his eyes. He turned away from Wednesday and Jenna, hoping they hadn't seen the salty shimmer.

Wednesday loved the way Tom lifted and held his three-year-old daughter so gently. The father-daughter scene tugged at her heartstrings. The simple moments in life were so precious. It was one of the things she liked best about mortals, their simple, wonderful lives. She and Jenna followed Tom into the house, Tamra following behind.

She didn't want to leave. She loved it here. She felt an instant connection to the little girls. She knew she could make a difference here. Lumina had been right. She was perfect for the job. Lumina never made a mistake.

They walked through the long hallway to the front foyer. Tom opened the door with one hand, the other arm still holding the sleeping Michaela snugly against him. Her little legs wrapped tightly about his waist, her lashes rested against her rounded cheeks like soft dragonfly wings. She sucked her thumb, her miniature forefinger rubbing rhythmically against her nose.

"Thank you for coming, Miss Green," he said, his smile warm. "We'll let you know tomorrow."

Wednesday gave Jenna's hand a quick squeeze before letting go. "It was nice to meet you, Jenna." She picked up her bag from the hallway table and walked out onto the porch. "I look forward to hearing from you."

"Goodnight, Miss Wednesday," chirped Tamra.

Wednesday turned and waved back at the five-year-old. Jenna stood in front of her sister, watching Wednesday with an expression full of yearning. Even without magic, Wednesday knew she'd won Jenna's heart.

"Goodnight," Wednesday said, her voice soft and quiet. She impulsively stepped forward and leaned close to Jenna. "I'm so glad we finally met. Your letter was wonderful," she murmured into Jenna's ear.

"You got my letter?" Jenna squeaked, joy lighting up her eyes.

"Let's just say I didn't answer your father's ad, darling," Wednesday whispered. She drew away and looked into Jenna's youthful face, the little girl's nose just inches away from hers. "I'm here because you asked for me."

"Like Mary Poppins?"

Wednesday nodded. "Like Mary Poppins."

"Wow!" breathed Jenna, awed by this piece of information.

"But it's just between you and me," said Wednesday with a conspiratorial wink. "Promise to keep it a secret?"

Jenna nodded, accepting the piece of paper Wednesday slipped into her hand with shaking fingers. It was her letter.

Wednesday was relieved to see Tom had missed the exchange. He was too busy trying to keep Tamra from tickling Michaela's bare feet.

Jenna leaned forward and touched Wednesday's hand with trembling fingers. Her eyes glistened with tears.

"I really want you to be our nanny," the little girl whispered. "But no one can ever be Mommy."

Jenna's sad voice caused Wednesday's heart to break. She gave Jenna's fingers a gentle squeeze.

"I'd never try to take her place, sweetheart. She's your mother. No one can ever replace her."

Jenna smiled.

Wednesday returned her smile. "Goodnight."

"Goodnight," whispered Jenna. She hugged the letter to her chest, a happy grin spreading her pink lips.

Wednesday turned her attention to Tom. He had his hands full.

"Tamra, stop it. I shouldn't have to tell you more than once." His voice was stern but the corners of his mouth quivered. Tamra giggled and grabbed onto his pant leg.

"Good night, Dr. Anderson."

He looked up, gazing into Wednesday's eyes. "Goodnight."

Wednesday, knowing the job was in the bag, straightened the strap of her oversized purse, gave a final wave, stepped down the front porch steps into the darkness, and vanished into the night with a wide satisfied smile upon her face.

****

Three days later, she stood on the wide sweeping porch of Dr. Tom Anderson's home with two oversized carpetbags in her hands and two meowing cats, one tucked securely under each arm.

He'd offered her the job and she, of course, had accepted.

She was excited but terrified at the prospect of working for Tom Anderson. This was her first real job after all, and it'd be the first time she would have complete responsibility and authority over children. Wednesday took a deep breath. She bit her lower lip anxiously and struggled to quiet the crying cats in her arms. She set the carpetbags on the floor of the porch, one on each side of her trembling body.

"There's no reason to be nervous," she told herself, trying in vain to quiet her nerves. "You've watched children before. You'll be fine."

Yes, she'd watched children before, her sister's brood. But she felt she had a little more power when it came to her own kin. After all, she could yell at them if she wanted and they couldn't fire her. She was their aunt. It was a lifetime connection that couldn't be terminated.

Inky and Jazz glared at her through slanted eyes. The cats were not at all happy about being flown through the air and uprooted from their home. They'd grown quite comfortable at her sister Tuesday's house and had adopted her two-story colonial as their home.

"You behave," Wednesday warned, suspecting the two cats were bound to get in trouble. They sometimes reminded her of the spoiled, troublesome cats in Disney's animated movie about the rich cocker spaniel who falls in love with a mutt from the wrong side of the tracks. However, Inky and Jazz weren't as vicious as those two sneaky, spiteful Siamese cats.

The cats looked away from her, but the meowing softened.

Wednesday took another deep breath, hoping her heart would stop racing so frantically. She placed the pad of one slim forefinger on the doorbell and pressed. The bell's chimes filled the porch and entryway beyond with a cheerful melody.

"Stop being so nervous," Wednesday berated herself, disgusted by how incredibly edgy she felt. "They're just children. You're trained and trained well. It'll all work out."

But when the door opened, Wednesday knew she

didn't owe her jitters to the three adorable little girls inside the house. She knew with one glance into Dr. Tom Anderson's amazing green eyes that he was the reason for her anxiety. He looked so incredibly sexy standing in a crisp gray suit. She wanted to drop her two troublesome cats and fling her arms about his neck, kissing him fully on the lips.

Wednesday gulped and squeezed her frazzled cats too tightly. Inky and Jazz hissed in her arms, moving lithe, flexible bodies wildly, trying desperately to get away.

"Hi," Wednesday breathed softly.

She'd never had a man affect her so much. She most certainly never met a mortal man who caused her toes to curl in her shoes, the blood to pound hard in her ears, and her knees to feel so jelly-weak.

Tom Anderson smiled, the corners of his eyes crinkling attractively. Wednesday noticed for the very first time the dimple in his right cheek. She wanted to kiss it. She felt her cheeks flame at the thought.

"Hello." He eyed her cats with trepidation. "What have we here? I don't remember you mentioning your fury friends."

Yeah, she felt sort of guilty about that. She hadn't wanted to jinx anything. Not everyone liked animals, especially temperamental felines like Inky and Jazz. Her sister Tuesday hated them and had nearly thrown a party to celebrate their departure. The family's poor dog, a timid beagle named Ed, had gone into hiding during Wednesday's extended stay. And Wednesday hadn't blamed him. Her cats were notorious mischief-makers, and they weren't particularly nice to the canine variety.

"They're my family," she admitted. "I hope you don't mind."

"No. No problem. My daughters adore animals. Come in." He gestured her into the front foyer, grabbed her discarded bags, and closed the front door with his hip. "Is this it?" he asked, dropping the bags on the tiled foyer.

Wednesday spun on her heel to face him, Inky and Jazz meowing in protest as she continued to clutch them much too tightly against her trembling body.

"What?' She tilted her head to one side.

Her heart fluttered as he straightened his tall body and smoothed out the creases of his expensive suit. He was handsome. He was absolutely charming. She knew not one warlock could come close to Dr. Tom Anderson's good looks.

He gestured to her two oversized pieces of luggage. "Is this all you brought with you?"

"Those and my two cats," she laughed. Inky and Jazz meowed plaintively as she squeezed them. She immediately relaxed her grip. "That's it."

Tom expelled a whistle and grinned at her. "I've never met a woman who traveled so light. I appreciate simplicity, especially in women. My wife was the same, except for her shoes." He smiled, the tender smile of a happy memory. "She liked a lot of shoes."

"Oh, I like shoes too."

He stepped around the bags and walked to her. "The children are still asleep."

Wednesday watched him move across the floor. He seemed to glide. She wasn't sure if a man could be described as graceful, but he crossed the space with masculine poise. The assured confidence of his long strides only added to the list of things she admired about Tom. Lumina had told her so much about him. Except, of course, how good looking he was in person. The little fairy's observations were invaluable. And one of Wednesday witchly gifts was that she knew people. She was able to read mortals. Her magical intuition told her there was much to like about Tom Anderson. He was a good man, loving and loyal, a lost man still trying to heal from a devastating loss.

"You might want to put them down," he suggested. The cats struggled madly against Wednesday's small frame. "They don't look too comfortable."

Wednesday was so involved with watching him cross the room, she'd completely forgotten about the two unhappy creatures in her arms. She loosened her grip and shrugged. "They'll be fine."

Inky and Jazz gazed up at her with yellow eyes and both bestowed an irritated hiss on her.

Tom leaned back, away from the wicked cats. "Okay, I admit I'm not a big cat lover. Dogs I can handle. Cats I'm not too thrilled about.

"My sister feels the same. As does her dog. Are you sure it's okay for me to have them here?"

His scared look was adorable. "Are they nice cats?"

"Most of the time."

He tilted his head to one side, eyeing the cats doubtfully. "Are you sure?"

"Of course I'm sure. They're my cats." Okay, so they weren't the sweetest animals, but they did like children. They preferred children. They were perfect familiars for a nanny witch. "They'll behave. I'll put them down when we get to my room."

Tom gave Wednesday a worried look as the cats sank their front claws into the cotton material of her shirt.

Wednesday gave a small twitch of her nose, causing them to stop clawing, hissing and struggling, instantly. Both cats, one coal black and the other silvery gray, went limp in her arms and started purring loudly. The amazed expression on Tom's face was priceless.

Wednesday tried not to laugh.

"How did you do that?" he asked, leaning forward and straightening his perfectly straight red tie.

Wednesday shrugged. "They're well-behaved cats, Dr. Anderson. I can assure you they won't be any problem. They're just a little bit nervous being in a new place and all. They love children. I promise."

He studied the cats for a few moments. "I guess I can understand their jitters."

"You can pet them if you want. They won't bite you," she encouraged softly. "I promise."

"I believe you. I don't need to pet them," Tom said, taking his eyes off the cats and turning his complete attention on her. Wednesday felt a delightful fluttering deep in her belly as his eyes met hers.

"You'll hardly even notice they're here," Wednesday said, sending a warning thought to Inky and Jazz to behave.

"I'm sure I won't, especially since I'll hardly be here. I'm seldom home. I work long hours, odd hours, and I work a lot of overtime. All reasons why I need a nanny."

"But I'm sure you find time to spend with your children," Wednesday said with a smile.

The smile immediately vanished. The look he gave her could've frozen Arizona's Sonoran Desert in the middle of summer.

"Wednesday, the one thing I do ask of a nanny is to not lecture me about raising my children. I'm a working single father. I make a good living. I provide for my children. I don't spend lots of time at home. I'd like to, but I'm not able to at this time. That is why I hired you."

Wednesday's heart seemed to stop beating for a moment. She didn't want him to be angry with her. That wouldn't be a good way to start her new job.

"I didn't mean anything by it, Dr. Anderson," she assured, hoping he wouldn't hold it against her.

"I know you didn't." He sighed, smoothing back the black curls of his hair. "I'm just very sensitive about the subject. I wonder every day if I'm doing the right thing for my children."

"You mean leaving them with a nanny?"

He sighed. "Yes. I love my girls. Only I don't have time to spend with them right now. I just can't. I feel guilty when I'm away from them. I feel guilty when I'm with them."

Wednesday's heart broke as she watched Tom's gaze rest upon a photo of his wife. It seemed to be the centerpiece of the long table lining the foyer wall. She remembered it from her first day. It was an 8 x 10 photograph, black and white, and it showcased Mary Anderson beaming a bright smile, her eyes laughing.

"I hope you understand and respect my decisions," Tom said so quietly Wednesday barely heard him.

Wednesday understood. She understood all too well. He didn't want to be around his children because it was too painful. Each one of his adorable little girls reminded him of his wife in some way, and he just couldn't deal with it yet. Dr. Tom Anderson was afraid to face the ghost of his wife so prominently reflected in the faces of his daughters. It was why she was here: to bring him back to his children who so desperately needed him and not a nanny.

"I understand," she murmured.

He was quiet for a long while, and Wednesday knew he was swept away into the past. She waited patiently, her heart going out to him.

Finally, he shook his dark head and closed his eyes. He took a couple of deep breaths before opening them again. A small, tentative smile curved his lips.

"Are you ready to see your rooms?"

Her eyes widened. "Rooms?"

"Yes, didn't I tell you about the guest house you'll be staying in?"

Wednesday shook her head. "No."

Of course, you'll be in the main house with the girls when I'm gone." He picked up her luggage. "Follow me."

"Follow me." He picked up her luggage and walked past her.

Wednesday readjusted Inky and Jazz in her arms and hurried after him as he disappeared out the back door. She could barely contain her excitement. She was actually going to have a place all her own. It'd been a long time since she'd had a place of her own. She was tired of living out of two ragged carpetbags at her sister's place. She loved her sister, her brother-in-law, and her nieces and nephews but everyone needed a place of their own.

She followed him out into the sunshine, struggling to keep up with his long strides. She lagged behind him, taking in the lush green of the lawn, the vibrant colors of the flowers waving happily in well-tended flowerbeds. Wednesday didn't mind walking behind him. She admired how he walked with the confidence of a man who knew his place in the world and the suit, certainly custom fit and expensive, fit his tall masculine body perfectly. It wasn't a bad view, far from it.

****

Tom led Wednesday to the front steps of the guest cottage Mary had insisted on. She'd planned to use it as their special getaway lover's cottage, tucked away in seclusion from the main house by draping willow trees and whispering aspens. Her romantic intentions had been good, but they'd never spent time in the cottage. When they hadn't been working together in surgery they'd been busy spending time with the kids. They'd never had much time for each other.

He still missed her terribly, even after two years. He set Wednesday's bags on the top step and dug the key out of his pocket.

"Wow!" Wednesday couldn't help but exclaim. "This house is adorable."

Tom agreed. It had a small porch littered with wicker furniture, a twisting sidewalk winding through abundant rose bushes, and it was painted white with black shutters and a charming red door.

"Do you like it?" He turned the key in the lock and twisted the doorknob, pushing the door open.

"Like it? I love it! Never in my wildest dreams did I think I'd have such a lovely place to stay. I'm not sure what I'll do with all the room."

It probably wasn't a good time to tell her he'd thought about bulldozing it down and putting in a basketball court. He glanced over his shoulder at her as he stepped inside. She looked truly appreciative and he was glad she'd be living within the walls of the cottage he never used. It needed a little tender loving care. He'd neglected it over the past few months. Actually, he'd completely avoided the place since Mary's death. The last time he'd stayed within the cheery painted walls was the night Mary died. He'd needed to be alone, away from the kids, away from family and friends. The cottage provided him the perfect secluded hideaway. Only his mother had known where he'd gone to mourn for his wife.

"Well, welcome home."

Wednesday smiled and Tom couldn't help but think of what an adorable picture she made standing with her two purring cats, one tucked in the crook of each arm. She looked fresh and young in faded denim jeans and a white cotton shirt. The shirt was tucked in at the waist, emphasizing the feminine smallness of her waist and slimness of her hips, and pink painted toenails poked out from open-toed leather sandals. Her coffee-colored hair was pulled away off her face in a loose ponytail, a few tendrils framed her face, and her cheeks were rosy with her own natural glow. She was beautiful in an earthy, wholesome sort of way.

Tom felt the unmistakable flare of desire. It was wrong to feel so, but there would be something drastically wrong if he didn't notice how sexy she looked standing just inches from him.

He could smell the lavender and lilac scent of her drifting from her clothing and body. She was refreshing and genuine, naturally lovely. His children's new nanny enchanted him. Yes, that was the word...enchanted.

"Thank you. It really is a lovely place."

"My wife decorated it. I think in her heart she always wanted to be an interior designer instead of a heart surgeon."

She walked by him. He leaned away from her, trying to avoid the cats. He still wasn't too sure about the felines. He tried not to watch the way the long tail of her hair moved with seductive grace against the small of her back or the way the denim of her jeans hugged the rounded flesh of her buttocks in molded perfection.

What was she doing to him? He shook his head, hoping to clear his mind of her. It was no use. He wanted to kiss her.

Wednesday spun in a small circle in the middle of the room. The cats meowed in protest. She set them down. They wasted no time running away, their tails arched high, the tips flicking back and forth in agitation. She smiled, a soft, sweet smile he knew he'd see in his dreams again that night.

"I absolutely love it," she gushed. She clapped her hands together enthusiastically.

"Good. It'll be your home as long as you stay with us. I'll need you up at the main house when I'm away."

"Of course."

"I'll show you the bedroom you can use on those occasions when I'm not here." He placed her two bags side by side in the living room. A professional chirping resounded from his beeper. He slid it from his belt, looked quickly at the number, and flipped out his cell phone. "This will only take a minute."

Wednesday nodded, turning away to give him more privacy.

His heart transplant coordinator was on the line. A heart was available for one of his patients. It was on its way, being delivered by air from somewhere in Wisconsin. He needed to get to the hospital. "I'll be there immediately," he said before flipping the phone closed. He placed the small device in a pocket in the folds of his suit. "I have to go."

"Emergency?" she asked.

"Yes. Heart transplant."

"Oh, how wonderful for your patient," she whispered. "The family must be over the moon."

Her compassion and concern for someone she didn't know was endearing and genuine. He liked her more if that was possible. And she looked so lovely. His heart tripped. He wished he could spend the whole day in Wednesday Green's magical aura. She made him feel good…she made him feel happy.

"I guess you'll have to get settled later. The children will be up soon."

"Do they have a schedule for the day?"

Tom gestured for her to follow him out the front door and back into the warmth of the sun. "Jenna has a riding lesson at eleven, Michaela a ballet lesson at two, and all three have swimming lessons at four. All the information is on the desk in the kitchen. Just call the kitchen Grand Central

Station."

"They have a busier schedule than most adults," she laughed, turning to face him in the midst of the garden of flowers.

Tom couldn't explain what happened next.

Something about Wednesday's warm laughter, her sparkling eyes, looking more brown than green, her heavenly lilac-lavender scent—something he couldn't quite define—captivated him.

He reached for her. His hands gripped her firmly at the hips, pulling her close.

Wednesday didn't struggle. Instead, she stopped laughing and Tom saw the twinkling light in her eyes vanish, replaced with something else, something heated—glowing and vibrant with need. Hot, steaming, scorching desire churned in his belly.

The feel of her hips under his hands drove him mad. He took a deep breath, laced his fingers in the loops of her jeans, and enjoyed the sensation of having her body close to his. He drew her nearer.

He should back away. He drew her nearer. She came willingly.

Tom knew he shouldn't kiss her. He was her employer after all. They didn't have a future together. But he how could he resist her? She was so deliciously charming, and she had a great set of lips. He couldn't wait to feel those lips against his.

"Wednesday," he murmured, gazing down into her upturned face.

"Dr. Anderson," she murmured back.

"Tom," he corrected.

"Tom," she whispered.

"I'm going to kiss you." His hands encircled her waist.

She nodded, giving a small gasp as he pulled her tight against him, lowering his lips to hers.

Wednesday melted like soft caramel against him, her arms reaching up across his broad shoulders, encircling his neck. She fit so well in his arms, as if she'd been made for him.

His lips slowly played across hers, sweet, warm, and enticing. She responded beneath his touch, her lips hungrily opening against his. Wave after wave of desire flowed through him and he didn't want it to stop.

But it did stop. Tom pulled away, realizing how wrong he was to kiss her. He had no right to kiss her, to put his new nanny in such an awkward position. She was his employee and he had to keep her as such. There couldn't be anything more than a professional relationship between them. Anything beyond that was impossible. He couldn't take the chance, no matter how great the kiss.

She unraveled her arms from around his neck and shoulders. He didn't miss the look in her eyes. Her obvious disappointment pleased him.

"I'm sorry." His tone was gruff; he was unable to meet her searching gaze.

"You don't have to be sorry." Her voice was barely a whisper.

"That shouldn't have happened." He looked at the sky, at the flowers, at anything but her. If he looked directly into her eyes he feared he'd kiss her again. "It won't happen again, Miss Green."

Her hand lingered against his chest. He felt the trembling of her fingers.

"But—"

"It won't happen again," he said curtly as he straightened his suit and tie with hands that only a moment ago had rested on the curve of her hips. "I think you can find your way back to the house."

"When will you be home?" He heard the hurt in her voice, knew it was his fault.

"I've left the hospital's number, my cell and beeper number, and my mother's phone number. If you have any questions feel free to call."

"I won't be bothering you, you needn't worry about me interrupting your work."

"Good. Take good care of my children."

She nodded. "Of course. Don't worry."

He spun on the heels of his shiny black shoes and walked away from her. He didn't look back.

Miss Wednesday Green was a whole lot of trouble. He shouldn't hire her. She was a whole lot of wide-eyed, raven-haired, long-legged trouble.

Trouble he didn't need, but trouble he had welcomed into his home most willingly.

Chapter Three

After two months of taking care of Dr. Anderson's girls, Wednesday felt completely and utterly exhausted. She'd never been so tired, emotionally and physically. She felt as if she'd competed in the Boston Marathon and came in last place.

Three little girls were a handful. Her training at the Magical Nanny University had not prepared her for three rambunctious girls. They were laughing, adorable balls of energy. She practically had to draw upon some of her witchcraft in order to keep up with them. It just went to show that all the magic in the world couldn't bottle up youthful exuberance. You only had it once, mortal or immortal, and once it was gone, it was most certainly gone for good.

And today, after a picnic in the park, a bike ride around one of the local lakes, and a trip to a nearby nature center, the three Anderson sisters were slightly subdued, their energy partially drained from a day spent in the sun.

Jenna was sprawled out on the floor on her stomach, reading a book. She'd indulged in a bubble bath and Wednesday had maneuvered her squeaky-clean hair into tight braids. The wet ends hit the white pages of the book, leaving wet, splotchy marks.

Michaela, also freshly bathed and smelling of baby shampoo, clutched her favorite teddy bear, her attention riveted by an animated movie. Her eyelids drooped every few seconds. She leaned heavily against Wednesday, her head bobbing against

Wednesday's shoulder.

Tamra's concentration was completely focused on putting a puzzle together. She twisted strands of wet curls around small fingers as she contemplated how each puzzle piece fit to make the picture of a kitten.

Wednesday could barely stay awake. She wanted to crawl into bed. She leaned back against the couch and closed her eyes. The clock on the mantle of the fireplace chimed the hour of nine o'clock. She opened one eye and glanced at it. It was bedtime for Jenna, Michaela and Tamra. She yawned. It was bedtime for her as well. She adored the girls, but she was ready for some sleep.

"Time for bed," she announced through another yawn.

"We're not ready for bed yet," protested Jenna, barely glancing up from the pages of her book. "It's still early."

"We've had a long day." Wednesday glanced at Tom's eldest daughter. She'd grown to really enjoy being with the seven-year-old. There was something enduring about her, something so likeable. She was a sweet kid with a lot of emotional baggage. She missed her mother and longed to spend time with her father.

Jenna looked up and Wednesday smiled warmly. "There is always tomorrow, Jenna"

"I'm not tired at all. Will we get to do as many fun things as we did today?"

Wednesday bit her lip to keep from laughing. Sleepiness made Jenna's eyelids heavy. She looked as if she was about to crash at any moment.

"Of course. Every day will be fun with me," said Wednesday cheerfully, making a mental note to get an energy potion from Dr. Alray, a warlock and potion expert who helped her family out of many unfortunate circumstances. She needed a mana potion to keep up with the bubbly girls.

"Yippy!" Tamra clapped her hands. "I go to bed now so tomorrow comes faster!" She scrambled to her feet, taking her puzzle and puzzle pieces with her. "Good night, Wednesday."

"Good night." Gooey warmth filled Wednesday's insides when Tamra placed a tentative kiss on her cheek before heading up the staircase.

"I'm still not tired," said a stubborn Jenna, looking back down at her book, braids swinging from side to side.

A delicate snore filled the room and Wednesday chuckled when she saw Michaela fast asleep.

Jenna smiled. "She always snores. Dad says Mom did too." Her smile turned sad, and Wednesday's heart lurched.

"Time for bed," whispered Wednesday. She lifted the sleeping Michaela and reached out a hand to Jenna. After a few seconds, Jenna closed the book, tucked it under her arm, and took Wednesday's hand.

They walked to the stairs, Jenna swinging Wednesday's hand between them.

"I hope you never leave," Jenna said softly as they moved up the creaky steps. "I like you very much."

Tears smarted Wednesday's eyes at Jenna's sweet words. Wednesday gave Jenna's hand a tender squeeze. "And I like you," she whispered.

She already knew she was growing far too attached to her employer's daughters. It hadn't taken long. They were far too precious not to fall in love with. It would be hard to leave them.

After she tucked the girls in, kissed each and wished them sweet dreams—casting a spell above each to make sure they did—she made her way back down the steps, practically tripping over Inky and Jazz lounging for some odd reason on the staircase.

She scolded them, irritated at the way they arrogantly flipped their tails in the air and gazed back at her with unblinking, slanted cat eyes. They obviously could care less about what she thought of them loitering on the stairs.

"Cats," she muttered with a shake of her head as she stepped over the two felines and continued her descent. She started to second-guess her answer to the favorite pet question.

The moment her feet hit the tiled foyer she heard the soft purring engine of a car followed by the sound of a door slamming. She froze at the bottom of the stairs, her hand tight upon the railing as she gazed at the closed front door. She heard his footsteps on the sidewalk.

He was home.

For a second she couldn't breathe. She stood at the bottom of the stairs, staring with wide eyes at the door, waiting for it to swing open and reveal the handsome doctor. She felt her heart start to race, the steady thump-thump vanishing and giving way to a more erratic, faster rhythm.

He'd kissed her in the garden on her first day, the memory still vivid in her mind. She hadn't seen him much since the kiss, and they'd not been alone again, but Tom had never been far from her mind. Who could forget such a kiss? Who could possibly forget someone as masculine, handsome, and deliciously wonderful as Dr. Tom Anderson?

That magic kiss without any magic at all, awakened emotions inside her she'd never even known existed.

The sound of the footsteps drew nearer. Wednesday discovered she was holding her breath. She didn't know what to expect from him. Would he treat her as his nanny or as the woman he embraced amidst the flowers that beautiful afternoon, her first day on the job?

The footsteps stopped and a key rattled in the keyhole.

It only took Wednesday a few seconds to realize she shouldn't be standing in the foyer waiting his return. It might look as if she was waiting, in hopes of pursuing more kisses and hot embraces from the lanky, muscular doctor.

"Fiddlesticks!" she cried softly as the doorknob turned and the door flew open. She snapped her right thumb and forefinger together and vanished from the foyer, landing soundlessly on the overstuffed blue sofa in the family room.

Wednesday reached blindly for the remote control as she heard the front door close, Tom's footsteps echoed in the hallway. The remote was nowhere to be seen, so she simply pointed at the television and it flipped through various channels until it stopped on a classic movie station. *Bringing Up Baby*, starring Katharine Hepburn and Cary Grant, blinked back at her. She curled her feet underneath her, conjured up a bowl of buttery popcorn, and glued her eyes to the TV, hoping she looked absorbed in the screwball comedy instead of on the man walking into the doorway.

"Hi." She waved the tips of her fingers at him. "How was the hospital?"

"I didn't lose any patients," he replied solemnly.

"The transplant surgery was a success?"

He nodded. "At least for now. Hopefully, there won't be any rejection."

"It must be rewarding, saving lives."

"It can be. Today was a good day." Tom loosened his tie. "They aren't all good days." Suddenly, he slumped against the doorframe, looking defeated. His green eyes darkened with sadness. "Yesterday I lost a little boy due to organ rejection. He was only eleven months old."

He looked and sounded exhausted. Wednesday's

heart went out to him. She didn't know how to respond, her brain and tongue couldn't seem to coordinate the right words. The guy saved lives on a daily basis. And sometimes his brilliant talent wasn't enough. One day he performed a miracle and the next day he was reminded cruelly he was only human with very human limitations. Even witches had limitations. They were not all-powerful. They couldn't cure people of illness or save lives. Some things were even beyond magic.

"I'm so sorry," she uttered. What else could she say? It was so horrible to comprehend. The death of an innocent child with his entire life yet to be lived was an indescribable loss, especially to the child's mother and father. And to the doctor who'd tried so valiantly to save his life.

Wednesday's heart swelled with deep affection for Tom. He was truly a remarkable man with a tender soul. And he obviously cared very deeply for his patients.

"I mourn each one," he said. He placed a forefinger and thumb on either side of the bridge of his nose and closed his pained eyes. "Sometimes I wish I'd chosen another profession, one that didn't involve sick children. I hate that I can't save them all."

"I'm sure there are countless children and parents who are thankful you decided to become a heart surgeon. You give it your best. Isn't that what matters, that you tried?"

Tom opened his eyes and gazed at her. Some of the pain faded. Some of the sadness disappeared, although Wednesday knew it would always be there, haunting just below the surface.

The corners of his mouth lifted slightly. "Thanks. I needed that." His stomach rumbled. His embarrassed grin broke the heavy atmosphere.

"Popcorn?" Wednesday asked after a moment of

silence. It was all she had to offer.

He glanced from her to the bowl. His stomach rumbled again. Wednesday smiled as she offered up her extra butter popcorn. A witch didn't need to worry about calories or cholesterol. It was one of the perks of being immortal.

"That actually sounds great," he sighed, throwing the suit jacket on a chair and crossing the room. "I haven't eaten a thing all day."

"And you, a doctor," teased Wednesday lightly with a shake of her head. "Shouldn't you know better?"

She turned her attention back to the movie. She tried not to dwell on the fact that despite a long shift in surgery, he looked good enough to eat. His suit jacket was tossed carelessly over one arm, his silk tie unknotted and draped casually around his neck, the top three buttons of his white dress shirt were undone.

Wednesday had the urge to undo a few more. She felt the heat rise in her cheeks.

Tom plopped down next to her and took a handful of popcorn. He gave her a sideways glance and grinned. "I should know better. However, doctors do make the worst patients. They also give great advice but don't take it themselves."

"Well, at least you admit it."

He laughed. "What are you watching?" He munched on the warm kernels of popcorn.

Wednesday told him the title as she reached into the bowl for another handful of popcorn. She jumped slightly when her hand brushed his. Electric currents radiated up and down her body at the touch of his skin. She turned her head and looked at him, not moving her hand from his. His eyes met hers. He leaned forward until their faces were only a few inches apart. His fingers curled about hers in the popcorn dish.

Wednesday couldn't look away from him. She felt herself falling into the mesmerizing depths of his eyes. Her heart hammered wildly against her ribcage. She felt certain he could hear it because the hurried beating was loud to her own ears and seemed to echo all around them. His lips were so close to her own she wondered if he might kiss her again.

She hoped he would.

"I want to apologize for the day in the garden," Tom said softly, his hand clasping hers gently. "I didn't mean to wait so long, but there never seemed to be a good time. I've been busy at the hospital and then there was the conference that sent me out of town for a few days. And when we're together we are never alone."

"Apologize?" she whispered, hoping he didn't mean the kiss, knowing he did. That's the only thing it could possibly be.

"For kissing you. I shouldn't have kissed you. You are my employee, and I had no right. Please forgive me."

She stared at him for a long moment, feeling disappointment fill every inch of her body. Her heart stopped running a wild pace, seeming to sink into the pit of her stomach. Her blood stopped rushing. For a moment, she felt as if the air had been knocked out of her.

He thought the kiss a mistake. He believed such a passionate and wonderful kiss a mistake.

Of course, he would. She should too. But she didn't. It had been too lovely to be a mistake. She'd thought about that kiss, dreamed at night about it, fantasized about it during the day. Tears pricked the corners of her eyes and she struggled for composure.

That kiss had changed her. Obviously, it hadn't affected him at all. It was just a mistake to him. By tomorrow, he wouldn't even remember it now that his conscious was clear.

Wednesday quickly pulled her hand away from his. “You are forgiven.” She forced a smile. “I haven’t given it a second thought. Besides, you already apologized.”

He looked surprised. “I did?”

“Yes, on the day you kissed me.”

“Well, I feel the need to apologize again. It was a lapse in judgment.”

“Of course.” She tried to smile. She didn’t like being referred to as a lapse in judgment.

“You are my employee.”

“Of course.” She looked away. She felt her heart breaking, which was ridiculous because she’d only just met him and couldn’t possibly possess such strong feelings for him. But she did.

“And I’m involved with someone.” His deep voice vibrated throughout the room even though he only whispered the words.

Wednesday’s eyes met his again. “What?”

“I’m involved with another woman. Her name is Anjelica Fitzgerald.”

He covered her hand with his. His fingers curled around hers. She didn’t want to pull away from him again. The heat of his hands sent delicious tingles through her body.

“I guess I should expect that.” The fact he had a girlfriend shouldn’t bother her, but it did. Very much. Far more than it should.

“Anjelica and I haven’t been dating very long, but we have a lot in common.”

“Oh?” She raised her eyebrows, interested in this woman who’d caught Tom’s attention.

“She works at the hospital, in the public affairs department.”

“Is it serious?” Wednesday couldn’t help but ask. She knew it was none of her business.

“I think it could turn into something serious.”

Wednesday gently untangled her fingers from his. "Have the children met her?"

Guilt shadowed Tom's brilliant green eyes and he looked away from her. "No," he admitted.

"Does she like children?" Wednesday prodded, knowing it was only a matter of time before he told her to mind her own business.

Tom shrugged. "I'm sure she does. We haven't really talked much about it."

Wednesday gave him an incredulous look. "Don't you think you should bring up the subject, considering you have three little girls?"

Tom turned back to face her and Wednesday knew the moment of questioning was over. She had overstepped. She had no right as his employee, as his nanny, to ask him such personal questions. She could see in his eyes he'd closed himself off.

"My personal life is none of your business, Miss Wednesday Green."

"Well, I think it is!" she retorted. She winced. What was she thinking? She barely knew him, and she really shouldn't care about his personal life. But she did care a great deal about Jenna, Michaela and Tamra. His personal life definitely affected them, and she was the only one who could watch out for them.

"You have no right." Anger laced his voice. He stood.

Wednesday jumped up from the couch, causing the bowl to tumble to the floor. Popped kernels of buttery corn rolled across the polished wood surface.

"It is my business. I'm the caretaker for your little girls, and the decisions you make in your life directly affect them."

"I don't need your stamp of approval." His hands clenched in fists at his sides. The black and white of the old movie flashed behind him, casting shadows on his face.

She knew she should stop. But she couldn't. "You hired me to look after your girls." Wednesday pointed an accusing finger at his chest. "I intend to do just that."

"You have gone too far, Miss Green. No one tells me what to do, especially not a beautiful, haughty nanny!"

Wednesday blushed and looked away from him.

A long awkward moment filled the silence between them.

When he at last spoke, his voice was soft, barely a whisper, "I shouldn't have mentioned Anjelica. I'm the one who brought up the subject. It is an inappropriate topic of conversation between us."

She turned her head. Her eyes met his. She felt she had to say something. It really wasn't her business. He could date whom he wanted. He was a grown man.

But before she could open her mouth to say anything, he reached out and grabbed her around the waist, tugging her hard against the length of his body.

Wednesday gasped, startled by the strength of his hands, the firmness of his grip on her hips, the warmth emanating from his body. Liquid heat swirled throughout her body. Honeyed heat flowed through her veins as she tilted her head back to gaze up into his handsome face.

"What is it about you?" he whispered. His breath was a soft breeze against her cheek.

"I don't know what you mean," she whispered back.

"You've put some spell on me." Tom pulled her closer. "This is wrong. So very wrong."

Wednesday's breasts crushed against his sinewy chest. She felt her nipples harden at the intimacy of their touch. She felt his heart beating rapidly through the fabric of his shirt. It galloped almost as fast as hers, but not quite. Hers was certainly winning the race.

She hadn't placed any spell on him. There were a few rules in the world of witches and warlocks, and one was you didn't mess with love. Witches and warlocks couldn't make someone fall in love, just like they couldn't cure people of life-threatening diseases.

"I can assure you the attraction you feel for me is genuine." She gazed into his dark green eyes. "It's not a spell."

"I shouldn't feel anything for you."

"But you do."

"I do," he agreed huskily.

He held her close with one arm and brushed away from her face the tendrils of her hair, tracing the curve of her jaw with the tips of his fingers.

"I shouldn't be doing this."

"We shouldn't be doing this," she murmured, closing her eyes, relishing the tenderness of his touch.

She wanted to kiss him. She leaned forward and brushed her lips against his, wrapping her arms about his shoulders and pulling him nearer. His lips moved over hers with hungry intensity, his tongue plunged into the moist recess of her mouth. Electric shocks flowed and ebbed through Wednesday's body in a steady stream as she leaned fully into the embrace, her fingers twining in the dark curls of his hair at the back of his neck.

"Tom," she said softly. She loved the sound of his name on her lips.

Calling him by his first name sounded right. She knew with certainty she was meant to be in his arms, and he was supposed to be kissing her. Her mother had once told her the magic of the universe selected a soul mate, just one, for every immortal. Immortals could fall in love many times, the same as humans, but they only had one true soul mate. And a person was very lucky if they ever found that special someone.

Wednesday knew she'd found that person. Tom Anderson was her soul mate. She knew it. There was no doubt, not a single one. Magic told her so. Her heart told her so.

The shrill ring of the phone cut their heated embrace short.

He pulled abruptly away. She missed his closeness. She wrapped her arms about her, her entire body trembling.

"We can't do this. It's wrong," he whispered. "And so much for keeping my promise to not have it happen again."

She reached for him. He didn't move away. She rested the palms of her hands against the base of his neck and laced her fingers together.

"Then why does it feel so right?" she murmured breathlessly.

Wednesday put gentle pressure on his neck, angling his head down towards her. She stood on tiptoes to touch his lips with hers. She fully covered his mouth with hers and kissed him tenderly, the tip of her nose touching his.

The phone continued to ring.

He pulled away. "I've got to get that."

Wednesday let him by. He paused at the doorway for a long moment, glancing back at her with his intense eyes before vanishing down the hallway and out of sight.

Wednesday sank down on the couch. She brought shaking hands to her face. Her cheeks were hot, her entire face flushed. Her body hummed from his passionate kiss, his tender touch, his warm embrace.

She was falling for him. And she couldn't. It wasn't allowed. She had a job to do. The children came first. Bringing Tom and the children together came second.

She and Tom didn't even come in third.

There was no *them.*

There never could be.

Chapter Four

Wednesday wisely stayed out of Tom's way the next morning.

She couldn't help but notice how flustered he was. He practically spilled coffee on his spotless navy suit jacket when she entered the kitchen. And he'd cut himself shaving. Tiny pieces of tissue stuck to his cheeks and chin. He also tried to avoid eye contact. He failed miserably.

Wednesday knew she looked great in her favorite pair of blue jeans and white tank top. His nervousness made her smile. There could be no doubt of her affect on him. It made her happy, even though it shouldn't. It'd be best if he didn't find her attractive, best for them both. She giggled after he made a hasty exit, mumbling good-bye, and kissing each daughter on the forehead.

She was positive she heard the squeal of tires against the asphalt of the driveway as the fancy sports car reversed out of the garage, around the circular driveway, and into the street.

"Daddy is odd today," Jenna observed, standing on tiptoe to look out the window. "He normally doesn't act that way."

"What way is that?" Wednesday asked innocently. She pulled away from the window, looking down at the seven-year-old.

"Just...odd." Jenna shook her blond head. "Weird."

"Well, I'm sure he just has a lot on his mind."

Jenna looked away from the window and up at Wednesday. "Maybe." She shrugged small shoulders and grabbed Wednesday's hand, guiding her out of the kitchen and down the hallway. "What are we doing today?"

It looked as if Jenna was going to have no problem forgetting about her father for the day. Wednesday didn't think she'd have any such luck. His dark hair and green eyes haunted her dreams.

Michaela and Tamra scampered after them, never far behind their big sister. They worshipped the ground she walked on unless they were in a fight or she was being too bossy. In those cases, they wanted nothing whatsoever to do with her.

"Yes, what?" Tamra asked eagerly.

Michaela, dragging her ragged teddy bear by one arm, took a break from sucking her thumb to shout, "I wanna play!"

"Well, I thought maybe we could go to the fair," Wednesday suggested. The county fair was in full swing and Wednesday thought it a great place to spend the day with the girls.

"Great!" shouted Jenna. She threw her arms about Wednesday's waist and gave her a tight squeeze. "I love the fair!"

"Me too!" Tamra cried.

"Me too!" Michaela repeated. She giggled, wrapped her arms around Wednesday's legs, and swung her teddy bear from side to side.

A great crack of thunder caused all four to jump.

Wednesday glanced over her shoulder and out the living room window. Splatters of rain hit the glass, lightning illuminated the darkened sky.

"Looks like we have to stay in. We'll go to the fair another day."

The three girls rushed to the window and pressed their little faces against the cool windowpane. After a few moments, they glanced up at her with such melodramatic dismay.

"Don't despair," Wednesday said cheerfully. She

fluffed their golden heads with her hands. "A rainy day can be even more fun."

The little girls didn't look convinced.

"We can go to a movie," Wednesday offered.

"To a movie theater?" Jenna asked, her eyes widening.

"Wow," Tamra breathed. She looked as though she'd been handed the moon and didn't know what to do with it.

"Wow!" Michaela shouted, giggling gaily. "I love movies!"

"Don't you ever go to the movies?" Wednesday asked softly.

Jenna and Tamra shook their heads. Michaela looked at them both before following their example, her curls bouncing.

"Not since Mommy died," whispered Jenna. "Daddy is too busy to take us to the movies or to the fair. He's too busy to do anything with us." She hung her head and sniffled.

Wednesday silently cursed Tom. He should be here for his children. They needed him at home. He hadn't taken any time off from work, even in the months following Mary's death. Lumina's report indicated he'd thrown himself into his work right away. The hospital had offered to give him up to three months off, but he'd refused. She was just the person to show Tom what he was missing by not spending some quality time with his daughters.

They ended up going to a matinee marathon for children. Three animated movies in a row were more than enough for Wednesday, although Jenna and Tamra loved it. Michaela fell fast asleep during the second flick and didn't wake up until Wednesday placed her in her car seat.

As soon as they arrived home, the phone rang. She slipped off her oversized purse, placed it on a nearby chair, and dropped the house and car keys in a small pewter tray on the long table. She tossed her slip-on shoes to the side and picked up the phone.

"Hello, Anderson residence," she said while she helped Michaela out of her bright purple raincoat.

"Wednesday." His deep voice echoing from the other end of the line caused her heart to stop for a second.

She hadn't seen him much over the past few weeks. And, when they were in the same room together, the kids were always with them, and the kiss they'd shared was never mentioned.

"Hello, Dr. Anderson."

"Where on earth have you been?"

Wednesday winced at the volume of his voice and held the receiver away from her ear. She shooed the kids into the family room and told Jenna to pull out some games.

"At the movies." She cradled the phone between her shoulder and cheek, pushing her purse to the floor so she could sit on a chair.

"For four hours?"

"Yes, a matinee marathon." She rolled her eyes heavenward. "We saw three animated movies."

"I'm surprised they sat through it."

"Jenna was good as gold. Tamra was a little antsy. Michaela mostly slept."

"Well, I'm glad you're back. Do you have a cell?"

The thought horrified her. She had cell phone phobia, actually technophobia. "A cell phone?" she squeaked.

"Yes."

She grimaced. "Most certainly not. I'm not a big fan of technology."

"I'm getting you one."

She held the phone away from her face and glared it before responding. "That's not necessary."

"I need to be able to get a hold of you at all times, especially if you are with my children."

He had a point. He was their father. "Okay," she relented reluctantly.

"I need a favor."

"What?"

She twirled the spiraled cord of the phone with long fingers. She wanted to zap him through the phone. He irritated her. He could use a good bolt of electricity. She could do it with just one flick of her finger. She stared at the tip of her finger and wished she wasn't such a chicken.

"I'm having a dinner party tonight."

"You need me to leave," she concluded.

"No. Do you cook?"

Wednesday stopped twirling the cord. "What?"

"Cook?"

"Sure. Kid favorites like macaroni and cheese and spaghetti," she laughed, "but I'm not a chef, Dr. Anderson."

"Well, do you think you could possibly fix something a little more elegant?"

He was getting more than irritating. She pointed her forefinger at the phone.

"It wasn't in my job description," she snapped.

"I can't get a caterer at such short notice and Anjelica asked some of the hospitals big donors over to the house tonight."

He sounded tired and for a moment she actually felt sorry for him. He worked hard all day and then his girlfriend decides to invite a few guests over for dinner. He probably wasn't having a good day.

"I can cook," Wednesday said, lowering her finger.

Tom's sigh was one of complete relief. "There'll be a bonus in it for you."

I'd rather you took some time off to be with your kids. And, give me another kiss.

She only muttered, "Great."

"We'll be there about seven. Set the table for

six."

He hung up before she could say another word.

"No problem. Absolutely no problem at all. I'll just whip it up," she mumbled into the empty phone line.

That was exactly what she intended to do.

And by seven o'clock, she'd created a five-course meal in the Anderson's kitchen, complete with chocolate mousse for dessert. An expensive Irish linen tablecloth covered the dining room table along with Mary's white Noritake china (well, Wednesday assumed it was Mary's), a charming pattern of green ivy gracing the edges. Candles glowed in crystal candelabras, causing the water in the tall goblets to shimmer brightly.

Wednesday surveyed her masterpiece and nodded in approval. There were certainly major perks to being a witch, materializing a meal out of air was definitely one of them. If any of the dinner guests or Tom found fault in her creation, she'd simply blink them to Siberia.

It'd be delightful to send snotty houseguests, including Tom, to Siberia. But before she could enjoy that thought too much, the front door opened and Tom's voice boomed in the foyer. She walked across the kitchen, stopping to give herself a quick once-over in the bottom of a copper pot before exiting into the hallway beyond.

She looked pretty good if she did say so herself. She'd taken a moment to create an attractive black dress; it hugged tightly to every curve she possessed. Just because she was the nanny didn't mean she couldn't dress sexy. Besides, she'd cooked up an amazing meal at the last minute. That took talent, even for a witch.

She stopped dead in her tracks in the middle of the foyer at the sight of the woman leaning on Tom's arm and gazing up at him with outlandish adoration. This woman clearly thought she possessed Tom. Ownership oozed from her.

Anjelica Fitzgerald resembled a porcelain doll. She had a perfect body, perfect hair, perfect skin, and perfect eyes. Tom and she looked created for each other, him with his black hair and dark green eyes, she with her wide blue eyes and wavy honey-colored hair. She wore a dress made of the palest blue silk, a color that enhanced the fabulous blue of her eyes; its neckline plunged low in the front.

Wednesday immediately didn't like the woman. It really had nothing to do with the fact she hung tight to Tom's arm and slithered her lithe body against his. Okay, so maybe her dislike for Anjelica had something to do with that. But what really unnerved Wednesday, what truly made her blood chill and foreboding creep through her entire body, was the way Anjelica looked at her with penetrating blue eyes, eyes void of any warmth.

This was not a woman who'd love another man's children. Anjelica Fitzgerald was the type of woman merely interested in obtaining a handsome, prestigious, and rich husband. She had no interest in his children. She'd spend all her days shopping, getting manicures and pedicures, massages and facials. The cold blue eyes scrutinizing Wednesday were far from friendly.

Wednesday froze in place. Anjelica viewed her as competition.

"You must be the *nanny*," sneered Anjelica. It was clear she wanted Wednesday to know her place in this household.

"Yes, I'm Wednesday Green." Wednesday held out one hand. "It's a pleasure to meet you."

Anjelica stared at Wednesday's offered hand as if it was covered with a severe form of leprosy. Wednesday fought the overwhelming desire to tell Anjelica she wasn't going to break out in hives if she shook it. After what seemed hours, Anjelica finally reached out one perfectly manicured hand. Her handshake was timid and weak. And this woman worked in public affairs at a major medical institution?

"I've heard so much about you."

Wednesday decided if looks could kill, she'd probably be lying in a dead heap on the foyer floor.

"Wednesday is extraordinary, Anjelica dear." Tom's smile was warm.

Wednesday smiled back, hoping he noticed how great she looked tonight in her little black dress. How could he not notice how fantastic she looked? The black cloth clung attractively and it was short enough to highlight one of her best features: her long legs.

"My children and I are very lucky to have her."

Wednesday couldn't help but beam. She also couldn't help remember the kisses they'd shared. She wished they were alone. She had an urge to run straight into his arms.

"As I am lucky to have you," Anjelica purred, tightening her hold on Tom's arm.

Wednesday watched with dismay as Anjelica leaned over and kissed Tom squarely on the lips. It was a passionate kiss, proving Anjelica was not all ice and snow. It was also a possessive move and Wednesday knew it. Anjelica was making sure the nanny knew just whom Tom belonged to.

Wednesday continued to smile, trying hard not to let the socialite see how much the kiss bothered her. It pleased her immensely to see how uncomfortable Tom looked drowning in Anjelica's affectionate possessiveness. His face reddened with embarrassment when Anjelica broke the heated embrace, wiped lipstick from his lips with one manicured thumb, and moved slightly away from him.

He avoided looking Wednesday in the eye, even though she stared at him hard. Did he not see what a snake he'd hooked up with? Probably not. Men were often blind when it came to deciphering women.

Anjelica turned to face Wednesday. "So, are you serving us tonight as well?" Her voice was so forcibly sugary sweet Wednesday actually felt sick.

"We can certainly serve ourselves," Tom said. "Wednesday has done enough for tonight."

"Well, she certainly can't think she is actually invited, darling," said Anjelica, her smile frigidly cold.

"Of course she is." Tom gave Anjelica a disapproving look. It pleased Wednesday immensely.

Anjelica's pasty smile grew colder and all color seemed to drain from her face. Wednesday tossed her one of her most brilliant smiles.

"I've already had dinner," Wednesday said. "I planned on serving you. I did make a five-course meal."

Tom's lower jaw sagged in surprise. "A five-course dinner?" he asked, amazed at her feat. "I certainly didn't expect that."

"Well, we couldn't very well serve the Piedmonts pizza and soft drinks, sweetheart!" Anjelica exclaimed with a high-pitched laugh. She looked relieved Wednesday would not be joining them at the dinner table.

"I had pizza and soft drinks for dinner," Wednesday said. "The children's choice. We ordered in."

"Ah, the children's favorite menu," Tom chuckled. "Are the hoodlums still up?"

"I believe so. They're in the family room watching television."

"You must meet the kids, Anjelica." Tom turned to gaze at his girlfriend.

The look on Anjelica's face was one of pure terror. She obviously had no intention of meeting the children at the moment and certainly had no idea what she'd do with them when she did.

The horror on her face was comical.

"Can't it wait?" Her voice actually squeaked slightly, her calm exterior quickly evaporating.

"No need to be afraid, Miss Fitzgerald. Just think of them as miniature adults," Wednesday said with a wide smile, her voice overly sweet. "I'm surprised you haven't met them yet."

Anjelica glared at her. Wednesday reveled in it. There was no way this chick was going to last in this household. Tom might be a workaholic and one of the nation's best surgeons, but he also loved his three little girls and he wasn't going to marry someone who didn't.

"I haven't had a chance to meet the little sweethearts yet. Tom and I haven't been dating for very long. But I can't wait to meet them." She curled her body against Tom's. Adoration lighted her eyes as she gazed up at Tom. "I know I'll just love them."

Wednesday planned on making sure Tom didn't marry Anjelica. The ice queen had no idea what she was up against. She didn't stand a chance against a witch.

"And I can't wait for you to meet them. They're going to love you." Tom placed a reassuring hand against the small of Anjelica's back. He started guiding her down the hallway toward the family room.

"But now, Tom?"

"Yes, now."

Wednesday followed eagerly behind, the high heels of her black designer shoes clicking against the floor. She wasn't about to miss Anjelica's introduction to the children.

Jenna, Tamra and Michaela squealed with

delight when they saw their beloved father walk through the doorway.

Jenna leaped up from the floor and jumped into his arms, giving him a big kiss on the cheek. Tamra did the same and Michaela gave him a timid smile, wiggling fingers at him and clutching her favorite ratty stuffed toy. Tom embraced them all in one huge hug, causing the three little girls to giggle. He rewarded each with a whisker rub, which caused them to shriek with joy and left their cheeks rosy and a little bit raw.

Wednesday leaned against the doorframe and crossed her arms in front of her. Her heart swelled at the scene. Tom definitely loved his children. She just had to convince him to spend more time with them.

Anjelica stood at arm's length from Tom and the children, staring at the three little girls as if they were aliens visiting from another planet.

"They won't bite you," Wednesday told Anjelica.

"I know that," Anjelica snapped. "I'm just not used to children."

"Well, you better get used to it." Wednesday walked by the rich socialite. "They aren't going anywhere."

The malicious smile curving Anjelica's ruby lips startled Wednesday. "Have you ever heard of boarding school, Miss Green?" Anjelica whispered. "Wonderful institutions."

Wednesday gazed back at her with astonishment.

"Dr. Anderson would never send them to boarding school," she hissed.

Anjelica waved one hand in the air as if Tom didn't really matter. "He's open to the idea, Miss Green. I'm afraid your days of employment are numbered."

Wednesday's eyes narrowed. "You aren't

engaged yet."

"All but announced," Anjelica purred.

It took all of Wednesday's efforts, not to launch a lightning bolt at the horrible woman. She wanted to destroy the triumphant smile, wipe it completely from the haughty face. Wednesday looked away from Anjelica to Tom and the children.

He laughed, joyous and vibrant laughter that crinkled the corners of his eyes. He smiled at Wednesday over the tops of the girls' heads. He gave her a charming wink. Her insides melted. She trembled, felt dizzy, and reached with shaking hands behind her for the edge of the table. She leaned her body against it, her eyes locked with his.

Anjelica moved in. She reminded Wednesday of a predatory panther seeking out her prey. She moved sleekly to Tom's side, placing her clawed hands on his arm and leaning close. She smiled at the children laughing in his arms. The smile lacked true affection and warmth.

Tom looked away from Wednesday to Anjelica.

Wednesday felt all the delicious warmth seep from her. She felt suddenly hollow and alone as she gazed upon Tom, his children, and the woman who might one day be his wife.

Chapter Five

Dinner with public relations guru Anjelica Fitzgerald proved to be a most interesting affair.

Wednesday's first impressions of Anjelica proved true. She made sure everyone at the table knew Wednesday was only the nanny, which translated into her being quite insignificant and unimportant. Wednesday tried to keep from using witchcraft, but in the end temptation won out.

With a flick of a finger, Anjelica's soup bowl tipped sideways, staining the blue silk of her dress an ugly orange-brown color. With a twitch of a nose, the straps of Anjelica's size 3 designer dress kept slipping down her bare shoulders. And when she stood up to propose a toast to the new hospital wing, the heels on her shoes cracked, causing her to lose her balance. The contents of her wineglass spilled all over the baldhead of the hospital's major philanthropist.

Anjelica flushed with embarrassment and glared at Wednesday across the table as if suspecting Wednesday was the cause of all her trouble, but how? It just couldn't be possible. Wednesday simply smiled innocently, tipped her wineglass slightly in acknowledgement, and took a sip.

Luckily, everyone at the table—except Anjelica—had a sense of humor and soon all the dinner guests were laughing. Anjelica left the table in a huff, wobbling with as much dignity as she could muster on the broken heels of her Versace pumps.

The guests turned out to be very nice people.

Wednesday hit it off great with all of them. She'd learned over the years all about perfect etiquette at a dinner table. She knew how to be proper in a social situation. It was only Anjelica who disliked her. And that suited Wednesday just fine.

Wednesday was glad when the guests finally shuffled out. At last, all was quiet. She sighed contentedly as she cleared the table, listening to the last car drive off into the night and the soft whispers of Anjelica and Tom in the foyer. She moved swiftly, removing plates, glasses, napkins, and silverware from the dining room table to the kitchen. She could easily listen to what they whispered about with keen witch ears, but out of respect for Tom, she chose not to.

She didn't have to use her special hearing. Anjelica's high-pitched voice echoed loudly in the hall.

"You have to get rid of her! I don't want her here. Get a different nanny, an older nanny. Send the kids away to school. Tonight was an absolute disaster and all because of her!"

Wednesday stalled between the dining room and kitchen, a pile of dirty plates balanced in one hand and four wineglasses held precariously between the fingers of the other. She held her breath as she waited for Tom's response.

"You can't be serious, Anjelica. The evening went great. Dr. McDonnell, his wife, and the Piedmonts are going to donate the money for the hospital wing."

Wednesday loved his deep voice more each day.

"How can you defend her?"

"Because she hasn't done anything wrong. She fixed us an excellent meal on short notice, which was above and beyond the call of duty, and our guests loved her."

Wednesday twitched her nose. The plates and

glasses disappeared, stacking neatly on the shelves of the nearby china hutch, clean and dry. She moved closer to the foyer, her feet not touching the floor.

"I demand you get rid of her," Anjelica said.

Wednesday had never heard a mortal actually snarl.

"The children love her. I have no intention of getting rid of her," Tom said firmly.

"But she is terribly odd."

Wednesday bunched her fists.

"Wednesday is...well, she's unique," Tom said softly.

What did he mean by unique? Was it a good unique or a bad unique?

Anjelica gave a very unladylike snort of disgust. "Unique is a nice way of saying odd, Tom."

Wednesday frowned.

"She stays."

Wednesday smiled.

"She goes."

Wednesday glared through the wall at where she thought Anjelica stood.

"She most definitely stays." Tom's voice clearly indicated the end of the conversation.

A soft stillness filled the foyer. Wednesday leaned her back against the wall and closed her eyes, straining to hear what Anjelica would say.

"But darling, I want to be the mother of those beautiful children." Anjelica's voice switched from demanding to sugary sweet. "I don't want a nanny."

"We aren't married yet, Anjelica."

"But we are going to be, aren't we Tom?" Anjelica cooed.

Wednesday grimaced. That woman couldn't be a mother to children. She was one of the most selfish, coldest, insincere mortals Wednesday had ever met.

"I'm not going to get into this with you right now, Anjelica. It's been a long day. Nanny

Wednesday Green stays."

"But only until we're married, Tom. I want to be with those children as much as possible. I want to be a full-time mother."

Wednesday wrinkled her nose. Tom couldn't possibly believe the vixen, could he? She raised one hand, wiggling long fingers in the air. Miss Fitzgerald needed a good zap.

"And a moment ago, you wanted to send them away to school. Good night, Anjelica." There was finality in his voice.

Wednesday lowered her hand and moved soundlessly along the wall. She looked around the doorframe and into the soft darkness beyond. Tom stood stoically, arms straight at his side. Anjelica stood in front of him, her hands resting lightly upon his broad shoulders.

"Tom, don't be mad," she purred sweetly.

"I think you should go home."

"I'd like to stay."

"No."

Wednesday watched in satisfaction as Tom placed his hands on Anjelica's slim wrists and pushed her away.

"Tom," Anjelica whispered. Her small pout and seductive smile made Wednesday want to gag.

"Can't I stay tonight? I want to stay every night. I want to be a family with you and those beautiful girls. I always wanted to be a mother."

Wednesday rolled her eyes. The woman was just too much. What was he doing with her? He could have anyone he wanted, and yet he chose a woman like Angelica. She just didn't understand it.

"Not tonight." He walked to the front door and opened it wide. Moonlight streamed in, flooding the icy blonde princess in light.

Wednesday's heart swelled with pride. He was actually getting rid of the little snow princess.

Angelica stood for a moment, her hands trembling. She still wore her ruined pumps, so she stood a little lopsided. Wednesday smothered an amused chuckle behind her hands, watching with delight as Angelica hobbled toward the door, her blue designer dress glimmering brightly in the moon's glow.

Wednesday listened to Angelica's whisper in the darkness: "Tom, we're still together, aren't we, darling?"

Silence.

Wednesday's fingers curled about the dining room doorframe. It seemed an eternity before Tom finally spoke. "I'm not sure, Angelica." His voice sounded tired and sad. "I'm just not sure right now. I do know I'm extremely tired, and I don't have the energy for a serious conversation about our relationship."

"Tom, I love you."

Wednesday heard the crocodile tears in Angelica's voice. She rolled her eyes. That woman couldn't possibly love a living creature.

"So you say," Tom sighed. He sounded so tired, so dejected, so utterly miserable, so emotionally drained.

Wednesday's heart went out to him. She wanted to run to him, take him in her arms, hug him, and tell him everything was going to be okay. Because it all was going to be okay. She would make sure of it.

Angelica kissed Tom overzealously on the lips. A tinge of jealousy unfurled inside Wednesday. Her only consolation was Tom didn't move into the kiss. He didn't respond. He continued to stand emotionless by the door, waiting for Angelica to leave.

"I'll see you tomorrow, darling," Angelica said, and then she was gone into the night, vanishing into the convertible waiting for her on the driveway.

Relief washed through Wednesday. The woman was finally gone. She only hoped Anjelica was gone for good from Tom's life.

She watched Tom walk out onto the porch. Her heart lurched in sympathy as he sat down on the top step. His shoulders slumped. He buried his head in his hands.

"Tom," Wednesday whispered. She wanted to go to him, but instinctively knew he needed time alone. She moved back into the candlelit dining room and walked into the brightly lighted kitchen, hoping he'd come to her.

****

Tom sat on the front step for over thirty minutes, pondering the situation with Anjelica and with the nanny living inside his house.

Anjelica's departure was a welcome relief. He'd just started to realize how irritating she could be. And she wasn't the warmest person in the world. She certainly wasn't Mary or Wednesday Green. She paled in comparison to their contagious warmth and joy and sweetness.

He sighed, leaning back against the white porch pillar. He couldn't stop thinking about Wednesday. She was so lovely. He remembered last night, their kiss, and the natural beauty of her oval-shaped face, how her hair flowed about her shoulders and down her back in dark, thick, glossy waves. She'd been dressed in a hot pink T-shirt and a pair of jean shorts, frayed at the edges, which showed off her long legs. There was something soothing about coming home to find her curled up on his couch. She was refreshing, intoxicating, exhilarating. And she made him laugh. He smiled in the darkness.

It had felt so good to laugh after a double shift at the hospital. There wasn't enough time to laugh doing the work he did. His work dealt with life and death. He missed coming home to Mary, missed the soft soothing words she'd whisper, missed unwinding at the end of the day with her. She always made him laugh and always made him see the brighter side of things. A person needed that when working in such a serious profession. Most of the time the surgeries worked and children survived, but not all the time. It could be heartbreaking work.

He still couldn't believe he'd kissed Wednesday twice. He couldn't forget, even though he tried. He wondered why he should care so much about her and that kiss. Wednesday was his children's nanny, but she was so beautiful, inside and out. Those eyes of hers, those odd, almost cat-like eyes, brown with flecks of green, seemed to reach deep into his soul.

Tom slipped out of his suit jacket, undid his tie, and unbuttoned his shirt.

He'd mourned Mary for two long years. He'd built a wall up around his emotions, protecting himself from the outside world, guarding his heart from another human being.

It wasn't what his departed wife would have wanted for him. She'd want him to love again. She'd want that for him and for their children.

Of course, he was dating Anjelica.

Tom smiled. He could almost hear Mary scolding him from heaven. She wouldn't approve.

Suddenly, he had the overwhelming need to see Wednesday.

When he walked into the kitchen, she was busy placing some pots and pans and into the dishwasher, the crystal and china nowhere to be seen.

She offered him a tender smile, her eyes catching his across the room. He leaned against the island counter, laying his palms flat against the marbled top. She tucked a few strands of hair behind her ears, closed the dishwasher, flipped it on, and turned her attention on him.

"Congratulations on your new hospital wing,"

she said softly.

The ticking of the clock on the wall behind the stove and the gentle humming of the dishwasher as it started its normal wash cycle were the only sounds in the kitchen for a few minutes as they stared into each other's eyes.

Tom shrugged one shoulder slightly. "The donation is a good thing for the hospital. Mr. and Mrs. McConnell are good people. So are the Piedmonts. They've donated a lot of time and money over the years."

"Did you like the meal?"

Tom moved around the edge of the island, closer to her. "It was absolutely delicious. It must've taken magic to do what you did tonight."

"Maybe just a little," she admitted. She leaned against the countertop and clasped her hands together in front of her.

He smiled and moved another step closer.

Wednesday looked damn good to him. The little black dress fit her body like a glove and her long, dark brown hair cascaded down her back in tempting waves of silky seduction. Tonight she seemed so womanly; so soft and warm and real. Anjelica seemed so hard and cold next to Wednesday's natural radiance.

"Does there happen to be any wine left?" he asked.

"I'm not sure," Wednesday whispered.

The house was silent around them, the only sound the vibrating melody of the dishwasher. The children were fast asleep. A soft classical melody played on the kitchen radio.

Tom stood in front of her, his body only inches from hers. "Would you share a glass with me?" he asked, gazing down into her upturned face.

Wednesday nodded. He reached toward her, his hands encircling her waist. He felt the heated softness of her skin through the flimsy fabric of her dress. He leaned in, his lips brushing her hair.

She smelled good. She smelled of lilacs and chocolate and that intoxicating lavender scent of hers, the one she always wore. The fragrance was an interesting concoction.

Wisps of her hair caressed his cheeks. Tom longed to bury his face amidst the shiny curls. His fingers wrapped around the neck of the wine bottle behind her. He wanted to wrap his fingers in the coffee-colored strands of her hair.

She closed her eyes. He loved the feel of her beneath his hand, of her hair against his lips, her body so enticingly close. She stood quietly, her hands still clasped tightly together, a barrier between them.

The clock ticked behind them. The melody on the radio changed. The haunting strands of Beethoven drifted through the kitchen. The notes circled about them softly, gently, lovingly. It was almost like an embrace.

Tom felt very romantic. He didn't know if it was the music or Wednesday's beauty or the fact he was confused about his feelings, probably a combination of all three. He chose not to think about it too much. He wanted to be in the moment. There was nothing wrong with wanting to enjoy being with a beautiful woman. Tom lifted the bottle and poured the red wine into two long-stemmed wineglasses.

Wednesday took the glass he offered. Her fingers clutched the thin stem. He noticed her fingers trembled.

"Thank you for your contribution to a successful evening," he toasted, tipping the edge of his glass in her direction.

"You don't need to thank me. I was happy to help."

"Wednesday, you put a lot of work into tonight's

dinner." He clinked the rim of his glass against hers, causing a soft crystal ring to echo throughout the kitchen; it was good crystal. "You impressed the guests and me. The meal was delicious."

"I didn't do that much," Wednesday protested, but her eyes glowed with appreciation. Tom admired the green-gold fire under her inky black lashes.

"You want to know something?" he asked, twirling his glass between his long fingers.

"What?"

"I like having you around, Wednesday Wednesday."

The entirely feminine sound of her girlish giggle caused Tom's heart to pick up speed.

"I like being around," Wednesday said. She took a sip of wine. "Mmmmm. That's good."

Tom wanted her. He knew it was wrong. At the moment, he didn't care. "Wednesday," he whispered.

"Yes," she whispered back, her tongue flicking across her lower lip as she spoke.

Tom groaned at the intimate movement of the pink tongue across the fullness of her lower lip. He leaned closer. He dropped the glass, not caring when it shattered on the tiled floor. Dark wine splattered against the white baseboard of the cabinets. He grabbed her small waist and lifted her effortlessly off of the floor, setting her deliciously rounded buttocks on the coolness of the counter.

"Wednesday, I think I want to kiss you," he murmured. The blood inside his veins intensified a few degrees. "Again."

Wednesday set her glass down and rested her fingers at the back of his neck, the soft tips gently massaging the base of his skull through his black curls.

"I want you to kiss me." She held his gaze boldly with her own. "I've wanted you to kiss me all night."

Wednesday traced the line of his jaw with

shaking fingers. The blazing trail of heat across his skin caused Tom's heartbeat to crescendo at an alarmingly fast speed.

He placed his hands gently on the small of her back and pulled her close. The length of her skirt shortened as she shifted closer, the black fabric sliding up her thighs gathered near her hips. His heart pounded rapidly in his chest and his breathing quickened as he leaned into her, his lips claiming hers in an ardent kiss.

Wednesday wrapped her arms about his neck and her legs around his muscled middle. Delicious warmth flowed thickly through his entire body as she fully and completely melted in his embrace.

She groaned against him, and he deepened the kiss, his tongue plunging into her soft mouth. She tasted of mint and chocolate and wine. She was scrumptious to taste and his lips moved hungrily across hers.

Wednesday moved against him; it drove him wild with need. He wanted to make love to her right there in the kitchen on the countertop. It would be so easy. It would all be so incredibly easy.

Tom's hands rested on her thighs. She shivered as his fingers walked up the soft insides of each thigh. She moaned in his ear, jumping slightly when the tips played at the edges of her lace underwear.

"Do you want me to stop?" he asked softly, tenderly.

She shook her head and slowly started to undo the buttons of his shirt. He watched her as she worked, his eyes never leaving hers. She slid the expensive shirt over his broad shoulders and down the length of his long arms.

"I never want you to stop, Tom. I love it when you touch me." She started to pull his undershirt from the waistband of his pants.

He sighed and kissed her again. She folded

against him. It felt so perfectly right to Tom.

And yet it was all so entirely wrong.

She was his nanny. Surely falling in love with her broke some ethical code.

Wednesday clung to him, burying her face against his chest. She started to cry. He felt the salty tears against his chest.

He held her gently, his lips brushed against her hair. "Wednesday?"

"I can't do this, Tom," she said softly, brushing tears away with the back of her hand.

"I thought you wanted it." He placed a hand upon her dark mass of hair. It was thick and soft beneath his fingers.

"I do." Her voice trembled.

"But?"

"But I just can't, Tom. I just can't."

She tilted back her head and gazed into his eyes. He lost himself in the brown-green depths, was startled at the emotion radiating there. Was it love? Could she possibly love him? But she hardly knew him. He knew nothing about her except what her professional references stated about her. And they'd given rave reviews. But how did he feel about her?

He didn't know if he really loved her. It was far too soon for that, wasn't it? He did know he had intense feelings for her. He'd never felt this way before, at least not since Mary. He'd never believed to be blessed twice in his life with such strong emotions. It was as if she were a part of him that had been missing his whole life. And he hadn't known what he'd been missing until Wednesday walked through his front door and into his life.

She brought laughter and sunshine and sparkle into his emotionless existence. She re-ignited the flame of passion and desire and love laid dormant so long.

But could he return the emotion he saw

shimmering her eyes? No. At least he didn't think so. He needed time to think, to clear his mind, to figure out what it was he really wanted.

"It's all right," he soothed.

He cupped her face in his hands and kissed the tip of her nose. His blood still pulsated wildly. His heart beat rapidly. A hard ache vibrated below his waist, one even a cold shower wouldn't dissipate.

"I'm sorry," she whispered tearfully.

"It would make things awkward for us."

"Yes." It was no more than a breath.

Tom gathered her closer to him, resting his chin upon the crown of her head. He rubbed her back and smoothed her hair. "This is the right thing to do."

She nodded. "I know it is. But why do I feel as if I'm missing out on something amazingly wonderful?"

His throat tightened. He didn't trust himself to speak. He closed his eyes and buried his face in the fragrant waves of her hair, rocking her back and forth in rhythm to the tune drifting from the old radio in the corner.

Chapter Six

Wednesday should have been prepared for a visit from Lumina, but she wasn't and the sight of the little fairy perched on the edge of her nightstand startled her.

"Lumina!"

The fairy stared at her with accusing eyes. Her little legs swung rapidly along the side of the nightstand and her transparent wings fluttered madly. She didn't look at all happy with her charge.

"You are a very naughty witch," Lumina stated. Her little voice shook with anger.

Wednesday winced as she struggled up to a sitting position. She smoothed hair away from her face and twisted the dark mass into a loose knot at the nape of her neck.

"I don't know what you're talking about," she said.

Wednesday knew she wasn't a very good liar. Lumina would be able to see right through her facade, but she had to try. She just couldn't admit to being in love with Tom. It'd be disastrous. Lumina would surely prevent her from finishing her assignment.

"Don't fib to me," Lumina shouted, her voice the volume of a human whisper. "I know exactly what you've been up to. You are fraternizing with your employer. Do I need to quote from the rulebook? Fraternizing is a definite no-no." She shook her finger for emphasis.

Wednesday feigned innocence in the face of Lumina's accusing finger. "I don't know what you're talking about, Lumina. I'm simply doing my job. There is nothing going on between Dr. Tom Anderson and myself. It's strictly professional."

Lumina rose from the oak nightstand, wings fluttering fast against her tiny back. She flew at Wednesday. She was an angry little fairy. Wednesday cringed and backed up against the headboard, gathering the sheets to her neck.

"It has to stop, Wednesday! It has to stop! Your duty is to those children. You have to make them happy. Once they and their father are happy, you're on your way, out the door, job finished. You cannot, must not, get involved with their father."

Wednesday grimaced. Closing her eyes, she leaned her head back until it clunked against the headboard. "Ouch." She gave her noggin a tender rub. "I can't help it, Lumina."

Memories of what happened the night of her magical five-course meal assaulted her. She couldn't forget how his strong arms wrapped around her, the feel of his lips upon hers, and the heat of his hands on her thighs, inching up and up and—

"Snap out of it!" Lumina shouted in Wednesday's ear.

Wednesday's eyes snapped open.

Lumina placed tiny hands on her tiny hips and shook her head. Her long coppery curls bounced against pale bare shoulders. The fairy dust sprinkled throughout her hair glowed in the sunlight drifting through the open window of the bedroom.

"I can't. I've tried. I can't stop how I feel," Wednesday whispered miserably.

Tears welled in her eyes. Her heart ached with worry and frustration. Her future was at stake. Being a magical nanny was all she'd ever wanted to be, and now her dream could be over, before it even started, if the Foundation discovered she'd been fraternizing with the children's father.

"You have no choice. We can't let this continue."

Wednesday nodded, brushing a tear from her cheek. "I guess I should pack my bags."

"I didn't say that." Lumina fluttered down onto Wednesday's right knee and sat Indian-style, cupping her chin in one miniature hand.

"I don't want you to leave our organization. You're a great nanny. We just have to figure out a way to make this work. We can't let the Board find out about this."

"Who's going to tell them?" Wednesday asked softly.

Lumina shrugged. "You're working directly under me, but there are always others observing, watching, especially on a first assignment like this. I only hope they haven't seen what's transpired between you and this doctor." She flung up her little arms in exasperation. "Wednesday, my goodness, it's only been a few weeks.

"He's an amazing man, Lumina." Wednesday couldn't keep the girlish delight from her face. Just the thought of Tom made her feel all warm and gooey inside.

"I'm sure he is. I know he is. But he's most certainly off limits to you. You have to remember that. You must remember that."

Wednesday snuggled down under the covers, making sure not to disturb Lumina from her perch on top her knee.

"I care about him, really care for him." She sniffled, rubbing her nose with the back of her hand. "I care for him, a lot. And not the way a nanny should feel for the father of her charges."

Sympathy flooded Lumina's silver eyes. "I thought as much." She pulled a small handkerchief from her pocket and offered it to Wednesday.

Wednesday took it, the tiny four-cornered piece of faery lace grew four times its size the minute it touched her fingers. “Thank you.”

“You’re most welcome.”

Wednesday dabbed the corners of her eyes. “It’s a wonderful feeling, indescribable really. I’ve never truly felt like this before. Is this what true love feels like?” She sighed miserably.

“Love is a marvelous thing,” Lumina agreed. “But it has its lows, its heartaches, as well as the highs, the joy.”

Wednesday nodded. “Yes, it is. Oh, Lumina, he is so amazing.”

“Yes, you’ve said that. And I already know it. I studied him. Remember.”

“Thanks for listening. I’m so happy to have someone to confess to at long last.”

“There have been many witches who’ve fallen in love with mortals. And the relationships have not worked.”

“Yes. But that isn’t always the case. My sister is one of the exceptions,” Wednesday said. She tucked a strand of hair behind one ear. “She fell in love with a mortal and everything seems to be working out for her.”

“Perhaps you should ask your sister for some advice,” Lumina suggested.

“She’s not going to be much help in this case, she’s a little biased in favor of relationships with mortals. She highly encourages it.”

“Tuesday’s marriage is one of the few that’s worked. Marriages between mortals and witches usually don’t last. It’s a sad statistic, but true. How about your mother? What’s her opinion?”

Wednesday grimaced. “My mother takes the complete opposite approach of Tuesday. She’s absolutely against the idea. Having one daughter marry a mortal almost made her have a breakdown. I’m not sure if she can live through another.”

Lumina sighed. “I don’t know what to do,

Wednesday. I can only protect you for so long. Someone is bound to discover your attraction to this man."

Wednesday looked out the open window. She saw the main house looming in the distance. Somewhere inside Tom was getting ready for another double-shift at the hospital. She wondered if he remembered their heated embrace. She flushed. She knew he would.

Lumina sighed again. She patted Wednesday's knee. The touch was so light Wednesday barely felt it.

"I'm worried about you, dear. I'm very worried. Can you stop this? You mustn't get any closer. The relationship could jeopardize your work here. It could harm more than just that."

"My entire life," Wednesday murmured.

"I think you should talk to your mother and Tuesday. Listen again to both sides. No matter what, you must not let this relationship progress any further while you are on this job. It could kill your promising career," Lumina warned.

"I know."

Wednesday felt sad, incredibly sad.

There was a knock at the door. It caused Lumina to flit about in nervous distress.

"I must go. Be wise, Wednesday dear. I'm warning you. I may not be the only one watching you. This is your first official nanny job after all."

Wednesday nodded, unable to say a word.

Lumina placed a light kiss on Wednesday's tear-stained cheek. "Be a good witch. I'll be in touch. By the way, you're doing a wonderful job with those children."

"Thanks."

The knock came again. It was followed by Tom's insistent voice calling out her name.

Wednesday glanced toward the front door, which

she could see clearly from her bedroom. When she looked back, Lumina had vanished, flying as fast as a hummingbird through the open window and up into the blue of the morning sky. She trusted Lumina to keep her secret, but she did worry about the other prying eyes the little fairy had hinted at. Wednesday had never thought much about the possibility that others would be watching her. She should've realized it was possible, considering this was her first job.

"Bye, Lumina," Wednesday whispered. She hopped out of bed and hurried to the front door, pulling on her favorite terry cloth robe as she skidded across the hardwood floors.

Her heart hammered, wild and erratic, in her chest as she flung open the door and gazed up into Tom's eyes. Oh, my, those amazing eyes!

"Good morning," he said.

He sounded nervous. He looked nervous. She saw it in the tilt of his smile. She smiled back, hoping she could hide her skittish nerves from him.

"Good morning."

Tom looked down at her with an intense expression. Wednesday saw the memory of the previous evening in the green depths of his eyes. She noticed no regret. She only sensed sadness. It mirrored her own. It broke her heart.

"I'm heading into work. I just wanted to stop by to thank you again for the dinner. The Piedmonts are still raving about it. You'll find a bonus in your first check."

"Thanks a bunch, but it isn't necessary." Guilt tugged at her conscience. She didn't deserve a bonus. She cheated by using magic.

"Yes, it is. I'm still daydreaming over the chocolate mousse."

He was dressed for work, looking handsome in a custom-made suit. It fit his body like a second skin.

He looked away, an uncomfortable silence filled the space between them.

Wednesday leaned against the doorframe. She wanted to help him but didn't know how. Her heart ached for him. She didn't know what to say. She didn't know the words to make it all better.

At last, his gaze rested again on her face. "You look beautiful in the morning," he said, his voice silky and low.

She felt the blush in her cheeks. She lowered her head. Soft tendrils of hair fell like a curtain against her face, shielding it from his eyes. His words were unexpected, appreciated, yes, but unexpected.

"Wednesday," he whispered. He took a step closer. Stopped.

Wednesday closed her eyes and felt the burning of hot tears. If love was such a wonderful thing then why, oh why, did it hurt so much? She started to lean towards him, wanting his strong arms to close about her, longing to rest her head upon his broad chest. She stopped herself, wrapping her arms tight against her body and stepping back from the warmth and shelter she craved.

She remembered Lumina's words and the faces of the children loomed before her.

"No," she whispered, keeping her head lowered so he could not read the expression on her face.

"Wednesday, I want to talk about what happened after your amazing five-course dinner."

She opened her eyes and watched her toes curl against the cream and burgundy rug. Her bare feet had never seemed so interesting.

"You already thanked me more than once."

"I think you know what I'm referring to."

Wednesday shook her head. "I think we've said enough. We need to have a strictly professional relationship."

"For the children," Tom murmured.

His fingers touched her hair.

She slowly lifted her head, the curtain of hair falling away, revealing her face to Tom. Wednesday knew at any moment a cascade of hot salty tears might splash down her cheeks. She knew the feelings she felt for him were transparent, clearly displayed in her eyes. She'd never been very good at hiding her emotions.

"For the children and for us," she said, her voice shaking.

Tom nodded. He took a step away from her and straightened his purple tie. She noticed his fingers shook. "I'll be gone until tomorrow evening."

"Have the kids been fed their breakfast yet?" She hated making small talk with him, hated acting as if everything was just as it had been before their passionate embrace in the kitchen that night.

"They're eating their favorite as we speak, blueberry pancakes."

Her stomach rumbled. "That sounds delicious. I didn't know you cooked."

Tom grinned. Wednesday's heart warmed. It was good to see.

"I didn't," he admitted. "My mother's here."

Wednesday's heart lurched. She didn't know if she was ready to face his mother.

Tom took a step forward and gave her arm a comforting squeeze.

"You needn't fear my mother. She's very nice."

"All men say that about their mothers," said Wednesday, rolling her eyes heavenward.

Tom laughed. His hand continued to rest upon her bare arm. She didn't want him to remove it. She wanted to be close to him and to have him touch her.

"Maybe so, but my mother is nice and she can't wait to meet you."

"Is she planning on spending the entire day with

us?" The heat of his hand upon her skin was distracting. She wanted to launch herself into his arms, to pull him inside the cottage, to kiss him and be held by him.

"Oh, I don't think so." He removed his hand. She missed its gentle pressure, its tender warmth. "My mother is an extremely busy woman. She always has some volunteer event to attend. Her visit is a surprise. She just sort of showed up unannounced."

"Does she do that often?"

"Not as much as before. In the months following Mary's death she practically moved in. She left on a European vacation with two of my aunts shortly after I hired you. She's been missing her granddaughters. Can you blame her?"

Wednesday smiled. "No. Absolutely not. The girls are adorable. I couldn't imagine staying away from them for very long."

"How about your mother? Should I be warned of surprise visits?" he asked.

Wednesday grimaced. It rather surprised her she hadn't received a visit from her meddling mother. She knew she would eventually. It was just a matter of time before Tuesday told Sunday where she was.

She shuddered "Let's hope not."

"Not a good relationship?" he inquired.

"Just wait until you meet her." Wednesday wasn't sure how to explain her mother. She was one of those individuals who couldn't possibly be described. A person just had to meet her in person to understand what she was like. She decided to simplify. "She's complicated. Let's just say she isn't as nice as your mother."

He reached a hand to her face, resting a palm against her cheek. She turned into it, resisting the impulse to place a kiss against his skin.

"I find that hard to believe," he murmured, his

voice soft, caressing. The pads of his fingers touched her skin. "She can't be all that bad. After all, she raised a perfect daughter."

His intimate touch caused her heart to pick up speed. Her bare toes curled against the wood floor. "You shouldn't flatter me so."

"Why not?"

"Because I just might stay forever," Wednesday said before she thought. She bit her lip, wishing she could take back the words.

He traced the line of her jaw with light tender fingertips. Wednesday shivered at his touch and the fire he ignited deep inside her flamed even brighter.

"Would that be such a bad thing?" His voice was as rich and soothing as hot chocolate on a cold wintry night.

She didn't trust herself to speak and could only shake her head.

His hand slipped from her cheek. He backed away. Wednesday knew he was reluctant to leave her. "Enjoy the morning with my mother."

"When will you be home?" Her voice seemed breathless to her own ears.

"I've already told you. Tomorrow evening."

That's right. He had. But she'd forgotten. His closeness, the feel of his touch had made that fact disappear from her mind.

"Why don't you come home tonight and take tomorrow off," she suggested. "The girls and I are going on a picnic."

Tom shook his head and glanced at his watch. He was already dismissing her and the girls, already in doctor-mode. "I have responsibilities, as do you. Go on your picnic and enjoy yourselves."

"There is a fair in town this weekend. Do you work?"

"I do."

"Take the weekend off. We can go to the zoo or

do something else. The girls would love it."

He turned away. "I can't. I'll see you tomorrow night." He stepped off the porch and down the stairs.

Wednesday hurried across the small porch after him. She didn't follow him down the stairs, standing on the top step. "You can for your daughters," she called after him.

Tom stopped, pivoting slowly to face her. His eyes turned hard, and the friendly, playful smile of minutes before vanished before her eyes.

A twinge of regret fluttered inside her, but she was determined to hold her ground. He needed someone to remind him not to forget about his daughters. His flavor of the moment, ice-queen Anjelica, certainly wouldn't. They needed their father far more than they needed her, another nanny, or anyone else.

"Let's not do this today, Wednesday."

She ignored the warning in his voice. He needed a little pushing. No one else seemed to be up to the challenge. But she was. "If not today then when?"

"I don't have time to be going on picnics or to the zoo. I have a very serious job that takes up most of my time."

"You don't have to remind me of that, Tom. I just thought it might do you some good to spend time with your children. They love you and admire you and want to be with you."

"And I love them. Don't ever doubt that. When they are older they'll understand."

"I'm older and I don't understand," she whispered. "Come to the fair, Tom. Come and have some fun. You are so busy saving lives you've forgotten how to live yours."

His body stiffened. "You've crossed the line. Don't forget your place in my home. You are my employee. You are my children's nanny. You are not my therapist. If I want advice I'll ask for it."

The color of his eyes turned dark, dark green. He was angry and getting angrier. Wednesday decided it was good for him. "And you, Dr. Anderson, crossed the line the other night. How easily you forget about my place in this home when it pleases you," she said irritably. She was quite pleased to see his lower jaw drop in astonishment.

"Wednesday, I—"

"Have a great day at the hospital, Dr. Anderson." She turned on her heel and raced into the cottage, slamming the door on his surprised face.

Chapter Seven

Tom's mother was just as Wednesday imagined. She was slim and trim with a short, no-nonsense haircut. Her nails were manicured to perfection. She was a person who somehow managed to make jeans and a sweater look elegant. Not a trace of makeup graced her face, her blue eyes were kind, her smile friendly.

"Hello," she said when Wednesday walked into the kitchen. "You must be the nanny I've been hearing so much about. I'm Janet."

She held out her hand. Wednesday shook it timidly. She wasn't sure how to act around Tom's mom. Just how much did Janet Anderson know about their relationship?

"I hope all good," Wednesday said.

Tom's mother laughed. It was a delightful sound, reminding Wednesday of a bubbling brook, rich, sparkling, and full of life.

"Most definitely."

Wednesday sniffed the air. It smelled heavenly.

"You're as lovely as my munchkins said." Janet gave Jenna's long braid a loving tweak and placed a plate of steaming pancakes topped with blueberries and whipped cream in front of a beaming Tamra.

Wednesday warmed to Janet immediately and instinctively knew Janet felt the same.

She smiled at the three girls and they grinned back in that innocent way only children could master. When she wiggled her eyebrows at them, they giggled, all three shoveling forks laden with grandma's cooking into their rosebud mouths.

"Would you like some of my famous pancakes?"

Wednesday nodded. "They smell divine."

"The kids love them. One, two, or three?" Janet asked, pouring fresh batter into a sizzling skillet.

"I'm starved. I think I'll have three."

"Nice to see a young woman with a healthy appetite. So many are on all these fad diets. I think it's so sad."

Wednesday guessed Tom's slim, trim mom had a great metabolism and probably exercised regularly. There wasn't an ounce of flab or fat on her body. Luckily, Wednesday didn't have to worry about gaining any weight. Being a witch had its perks.

"I never worry about things like that," Wednesday said.

Janet smiled. "I like you already."

"Yummy, Grandma," Tamra complimented through a mouthful of blueberries and soggy pancake.

"Don't talk with your mouth full," Janet gently scolded as she flipped over a perfectly circular cake.

"Yum! Yum!" crowed Michaela.

Wednesday laughed. A rather large dollop of whipped cream decorated Michaela's nose. She picked up a napkin and removed the fluffy mound with a quick flourish of a hand.

"Grandma, Wednesday likes peanut butter sandwiches with bananas just like us."

"Well, Jenna, then I guess she's just perfect for this family."

Janet started another pancake. "It sounds as if you are just perfect, a genuine Mary Poppins."

Wednesday flushed. "I don't think anyone could be Mary Poppins, after all wasn't she practically perfect in every way?"

Jenna squealed with laughter. Tamra, in a fit of amused giggles, spewed milk from her nose. And little Michaela tossed a few blueberries across the room. The berries dropped to the floor and fell to the mercy of Inky and Jazz, both of whom just happened to adore berries of any kind. Wednesday always knew she'd adopted two very odd felines.

"Well, that wasn't very ladylike now was it?" Janet asked.

Wednesday exchanged a merry look with Tom's mother while helping Tamra to clean up.

"Milk came out of my nose!" she laughed gleefully.

Wednesday chortled. "You seem awfully proud of it."

"Wait until I tell Daddy!"

"I'm sure he'll be sooooo proud," Jenna sighed in exasperation.

"Will you be staying with us all day?" Wednesday asked as Janet placed the plate of pancakes in front of Wednesday.

"I've got oodles to do, so I can't stay long. However, if you ever need a day off, just give me a call." Janet glanced over at the refrigerator. "I see my number is plastered in a place of honor."

"You are always welcome, Mrs. Anderson."

"Please call me Janet."

"And call me Wednesday."

Janet leaned over and gave Wednesday's hand a gentle squeeze. "I think we shall be great friends."

Wednesday couldn't agree more. She plunged her fork into the mouth-watering mountain of cakes. "Prize-winning," she complimented after swallowing a delicious bite and taking a drink of milk.

Janet smiled her thanks as she wiped Michaela's sticky mouth and face clean with a damp washcloth, and asked, "So, what's on the agenda today?"

"We're going on a picnic," Jenna supplied. She patted her mouth clean with a napkin, just like a perfect little lady, and asked to be excused from the table.

"You may," Janet told her independent granddaughter, "if you take your sisters with you."

"Do I have to?"

Wednesday detected a slight whine in Jenna's normally mature little voice.

Janet wagged her finger at her eldest granddaughter. "Yep. It's your job as the older sister to look after them."

"Wish I wasn't the oldest," grumbled Jenna as she helped Tamra down from her chair.

The two sisters held hands and meandered out of the kitchen. Baby Michaela waddled after them, dragging her raggedy teddy bear behind her. Inky and Jazz loped behind the trio, batting at the limp bear's stuffed limbs with a playful paw.

"Darlings," Janet sighed.

"Absolutely," agreed Wednesday.

She took another bite of Janet's fantastic pancakes.

"My son hasn't taken much time off from work since the time of Mary's funeral." Janet's eyes locked with Wednesday's. "Do you think he works too much?"

Wednesday decided honesty was the best policy with Janet. "Dr. Anderson is a workaholic. He gives very little time to his daughters." Wednesday swallowed the last of her pancakes and added, "He does love them, but I think he's avoiding them."

Janet sat down in the chair vacated by Jenna. "They remind him of her."

"I know," Wednesday said, her voice soft and filled with compassion. "I've seen the photos. They resemble her greatly. What was she like?"

A sorrowful smile twisted Janet's lips. "She was a wonderful person, a brilliant doctor, a loving wife, and a devoted mother. She gave up her career as a surgeon after Tamra was born. When she died, my son gave up on ever being happy again."

The agony Janet felt for her son was evident in her blue eyes. Her hands shook. Wednesday covered them with hers.

"He'll come around."

"You know, he doesn't have surgeries every day. Most of the time he's in meetings. He is involved in almost every aspect of that hospital, every committee, trying to stay away from home," Janet said, glancing about the large kitchen.

Wednesday nodded. "I asked him to go with us today, but he refused. Work reasons again."

Janet rested her chin in the palm of one hand. "You're a sweet girl. You take such good care of my little ones, but I'm afraid no one can help Tom."

"You may be surprised," Wednesday said as she plopped another piece of pancake in her mouth. It was good, the best she'd ever tasted. She wondered if Janet would share her recipe.

"It isn't that he can't take time off. He has plenty of vacation piled up."

Wednesday plunged her fork into the last few bites. She twirled the utensil loaded with syrup-laden cake in Janet's direction. "And he should take it." She plopped the scrumptious pile of cake tidbits into her mouth.

"But he won't." Janet sighed. She sounded so forlorn. The teakettle on the stove whistled. She stood and crossed the tiled floor, lifting the bright red kettle off the gas burner. She turned back to Wednesday. "Would you like a cup?"

"Yes, thank you."

"I appreciate your concern, but I'm starting to think my son is a lost cause." Janet poured hot water into a cup and offered it to Wednesday.

Wednesday accepted the cup. She grabbed a blueberry-flavored teabag out of the variety pack on the table, sprinkled a teaspoon of sugar, and added a few drops of milk into the hot liquid.

"He just needs a nudge," she assured Janet, keeping her tone cheerful. She didn't think he was a lost cause. In fact, she knew he wasn't.

Janet poured another cup. "I've tried..." She swirled a spoon between forefinger and thumb. "...but failed miserably. The entire family has failed to convince him of the importance of spending time with his girls. Mary would be horrified to see what he has become.

"He used to always put his family first. Every vacation day and personal day and sick day was given to his wife and daughters. And then Mary died, and he never recovered. Then, he dove into work with a vengeance."

Janet squeezed Wednesday's hand. "I wasn't very happy about him hiring another nanny. I even tried to do it myself after the last one. I thought I could do it all, but I've changed my mind. I think you might be just what he needs."

Wednesday felt her cheeks grow hot under Janet's gaze. She returned Janet's affectionate squeeze and withdrew her hand. "I'm not sure what you mean."

"The kids love you, Tom clearly thinks quite highly of you," Janet said and cupped her teacup in both hands, "and I like you."

"Thanks."

"I really do."

"Thanks again."

They sipped tea in companionable silence for a few minutes.

"I asked him to go to the zoo and the fair this weekend," Wednesday admitted. She couldn't resist sharing.

Hope sparkled in Janet's eyes.

Wednesday shook her head.

"I'll try working on him," Janet said. She added

another spoonful of sugar to her tea. "You get on him about the zoo, and I'll push for the carnival. He's bound to give in to one of us."

"Most likely you."

Janet's eyes twinkled at Wednesday. "I'm not so sure about that."

"I'm his paid employee. I don't think he cares much what I think."

Janet studied Wednesday for so long Wednesday grew quite uncomfortable. "I think he cares a great deal about you, Wednesday," she said at last.

"Really?" Wednesday winced at the hopeful sound in her voice. The last thing she needed was for Tom's mom to think there was something going on between them.

"Yeah, I do think so," Janet whispered. The knowing look in Janet's eyes made Wednesday feel uneasy. She tried to look disinterested and stared into her teacup, thankful when the shrill ring of the phone broke the awkward silence.

The sound of pattering feet filled the hallway as the girls hurried to grab the phone.

"Hello," Jenna yelled loudly. "Hiya, Daddy. Yep. Yep. Good. Tamra blew milk out her nose. I laughed. Michaela threw blueberries, and the cats ate them. Grandma's here. Do you want to talk to her? Okay. Wednesday, Daddy wants to talk to you."

"I wonder what he wants?" she asked to no one in particular. "I hope he doesn't want me to make another five-course dinner."

"I heard about that," said Janet. "However did you manage?"

Wednesday shrugged. "I have an uncle who's a chef. I picked up some pointers from him."

It wasn't exactly a lie. Her Uncle Eddie was head chef at a famous restaurant in London. But he didn't actually make the food himself. Nope. He added a whole lot of magic, which was why no one in the world could replicate his tantalizing recipes. It was deceptive, but the world hardly cared. Everyone traveling Europe knew of his restaurant, *Magical Flavor*, and made sure to make it a necessary stop.

Wednesday left the kitchen before Janet could ask questions about Uncle Eddie. She wasn't quite ready to explain her family to Tom's mother. Heck, she wasn't ready to explain her eccentric uncles, aunts, and cousins to anyone. There were plenty of them to talk about since no one ever died. Well, at least not for a very long, long time. A witch's lifespan was unusually long by mortal standards, covering many human lifetimes.

"Goodbye, Daddy," Jenna shouted into the phone.

Wednesday imagined Tom wincing at the other end of the line. Jenna's high-pitched shout could cause severe damage an eardrum. Cataloguing the little girl's behavior, she decided Jenna needed to learn a few things about phone etiquette. She took the receiver from the seven-year-old and shooed the chattering siblings out to the family room.

"This better not be about another dinner," she teased softly.

To Wednesday's complete surprise, Tom laughed. "Hi." His voice was warm, friendly, and he actually sounded, dare she say it, happy?

Her heart fluttered, hopefully. "Hi, to you, too."

"Hey, does the offer still stand?"

"For what?" His exuberance dumbfounded her.

"For the picnic."

"You want to come to the picnic?" she asked in amazement.

"Yes. I've changed my mind. I hope you still want me."

Wednesday's reflection in the mirror on the opposite wall showed her surprise. Her mouth hung open so wide she was sure a fly would buzz in. She snapped it shut.

"Well, am I still invited?" he asked.

He was incredibly cheerful. What in the world had come over him? What had happened to him on the way to the hospital?

She managed a whispered, "Of course."

"Great. Should I meet you at the park around noon?"

She clutched the receiver so tight her hands tingled. He wanted to come. She could barely squeak out an answer. But she managed, "Sounds perfect."

"The girls still like the one by our house best?"

"Yes."

"Good. See you at the park."

The line went dead.

Wednesday sat there for a good five minutes with the phone dangling from her ear. What had just happened? She hadn't cast a spell. Had she? She mumbled under her breath, "What on earth—?"

"What did Tom have to say?" Janet asked.

Wednesday removed the phone from her ear. She glanced up at Janet and shook her head, still somewhat stunned, with amazement. "You won't believe it. He says he's going with us."

"On the picnic?"

"Yes."

"Yippy!" Janet trilled.

Wednesday was startled to hear such a childish exclamation escape Janet's lips.

"Wednesday, my dear, you're already using your charms to work wonders on my Tom."

But I didn't even use magic to change his mind.

This was all very confusing.

"You're an angel sent from heaven, Wednesday Green," Janet exclaimed happily as she engulfed Wednesday in a hug.

Wednesday patted her back, absently. Why would Tom do a complete one-eighty?

"I'll still work on him about this weekend, but this is fabulous news."

"Yes, fabulous," Wednesday whispered.

Janet hurried down the hall. Wednesday heard her tell the news to the girls. The girls cheered, their sweet mirth causing Wednesday's heart to constrict.

"He's far too stubborn to change his mind just like that," Wednesday murmured aloud.

And then she heard laughter, soft, light, and joyous, and only a witch could hear it.

"Lumina," Wednesday looked about for the mischievous fairy, "where are you?"

She received no answer. Lumina either chose to remain very quiet or had wisely returned to the magical world.

Wednesday couldn't help but smile.

It looked as if Lumina was a romantic at heart.

****

Three hours later, she pulled up at the kids' favorite park, still rather bewildered by what had happened, but just as thrilled as the girls were when she saw Tom stride toward them with a huge, adorable, lopsided smile.

"Hi, gals," Tom exclaimed, opening the back door of the Ford Escape and releasing a giddy Michaela from her safety seat. "How's the Nanny Mobile?"

"No complaints." Wednesday turned off the ignition, watching Tom in the rearview mirror as he helped Tamra from the SUV.

He looked good. He'd discarded his suit and tie for jeans and a T-shirt, replacing his shiny dress shoes with comfortable running shoes.

Boy, Lumina had done a number on him.

"So, what's for lunch?"

She slipped out the driver's door, grabbed the basket of food, and answered, "Fried chicken and potato salad of course. What else?"

Wednesday's heart stopped beating when he

turned his gorgeous smile on her. He had a million-watt smile—too bad he seldom turned it on.

I owe you one, Lumina. Thanks for giving him a push.

"We want to go play. Can we, Daddy?" Jenna asked.

Tom chuckled. She jumped up and down with excitement, waving a frantic hand at a friend she'd spotted on the jungle gym.

"Have fun, but don't wander too far."

Jenna bounced off faster than a jackrabbit, with Tamra racing after her. When Michaela teetered in their direction Tom said, "Not so fast, kiddo."

He swept his youngest child up in his arms and tossed her in the air. He caught her in a loving hug and kissed the top of her wild curls. Michaela squealed with delight.

Wednesday carried the wicker picnic basket beside him. As Tom reached to take the load from her, his hand brushed against hers. "Here, I can take that."

She enjoyed the touch of his fingers light on the back of her hand. "It's all right. I can carry it."

"I insist." His green eyes sparkled.

Wednesday had never seen him so relaxed. Okay, this had to be more than a spell. Lumina's incantation might have convinced him to meet them for lunch, but it would have worn off by now. Fairy magic might be effective, but it expired quickly.

"Okay, thanks." She released her grip on the basket and put her hands on her hips. "But tell me what's really going on here."

"There's nothing to tell. It's simple." He placed a kiss on Michaela's cherubic cheek. She giggled, kissing her father back, with a sweet wet one on the lips. He laughed. "I wanted to see my girls."

They were adorable together. Wednesday's heart clenched. "But this morning you refused to join us or take the weekend off. As I recall, you were very adamant about it."

"I still can't take the weekend off."

"Oh?"

"Nope."

"I'm sorry to hear that, but you're here now. This is good."

His crooked smile was endearing.

"You're in an extremely good mood. A far cry from this morning."

He grimaced, looking just a tiny bit embarrassed. "I'm sorry about that."

She frowned at him. "How sorry are you?"

"Very." He adjusted a gurgling Michaela on his hip. She wrapped her arms about his neck and hugged him.

Wednesday couldn't help but grin. "Apology accepted."

He looked relieved.

"But I still want to know why you changed your mind. It had to be more than just wanting to see the girls. I mean—"

"How my attitude is so vastly different?" He shrugged. "No idea. One minute I'm typing away at emails, and the next, I'm feeling overly happy and enthused about a picnic in the park. It was a strange euphoric feeling. I can't explain why it happened or how quick it came on. You wouldn't believe me if I told you."

She touched his arm. "I might surprise you."

They turned together and starting walking towards the playground.

Tom was silent as they strolled arm and arm.

"Well, are you going to share?" Wednesday asked.

"Let's just say I felt loads of guilt, and I had the overwhelming sensation to spend some quality time with my daughters."

She hugged his arm tight against her. "Good."

He smiled at her. "Okay, I deserve that."

Wednesday returned his smile. "Yes, you did." She pulled her arm from his and tugged out a blanket from her bag. She draped it over one arm.

"Know of a good spot?" Tom asked.

"Over there by the willow tree." Wednesday looked around and found the perfect spot. She pointed at the oversized weeping willow at the north edge of the play equipment.

Wednesday took the lead. She wondered if he thought she was pretty. She didn't feel very attractive dressed in frayed pink shorts and the white tank top, both covered with black and silver cat hair. She'd piled her hair high, secured the dark mass with a variety of pastel clips, a bunch of stubborn strands cascaded down her neck and curled against her face.

"I just had to come," he said as Wednesday spread out the blanket under the refreshing shade.

She plucked Michaela from his arms. "The girls are very happy you're here."

Tom reached over and grabbed her hand.

Wednesday looked into his eyes.

"What about you? Are you happy to see me?"

"I invited you, didn't I?"

"For them?" He gestured at Jenna and Tamra immersed in the tractor tire swing.

"Yes, for them. I am the nanny. I want what's best for them." Wednesday pulled her hand from his. She almost wished he hadn't come. Being this close to him was unnerving.

Tom set the picnic hamper on the grass, opened it, and started to unpack it.

"Should I apologize again?" he asked.

"Not necessary."

"Friends?"

Wednesday sank down on the blanket with

Michaela. For a while, she didn't respond. She dared not look into his eyes. She busied herself organizing Michaela's jumble of toys. Michaela released a happy shriek, gazing with wide eyes at the smorgasbord of goodies, completely oblivious to grown-up conversation.

"Friends," Wednesday agreed at last.

His warm smile made her toes curl. "So, did you like her?"

Wednesday blinked at him. "Her? Whom are you talking about?" He couldn't be referring to that she-devil Anjelica.

"My mother," he supplied, noting her confusion.

I'm an idiot. No, I'm just an imbecile when I'm around him. My brain turns to mush around him.

"She's lovely, Tom. I enjoyed talking with her very much."

"She misses the girls. She practically moved in after the last nanny left to get married. She wasn't too keen on me hiring another one. We went for a long time without a nanny with Mom trying to do it all."

"She mentioned something like that."

Tom groaned. "I hope she wasn't too much a nuisance."

"Not at all," Wednesday replied and meant it. Janet Anderson was someone she saw herself capable of being friends with. "She was friendly and sweet and cares very much for you and her granddaughters. You're lucky to have a mother like Janet."

"Yeah, I guess." He tossed a seedless grape into his mouth and munched on it for a few seconds. "Sometimes, I think she sticks her nose in where it doesn't belong."

"All mothers do that."

"Does yours?" he asked.

Wednesday was silent. She wasn't sure how to

explain her unique mother. It wasn't just the fact she was a witch. Her mother was one of the most domineering, selfish, interfering mothers in all witchdom. If there were an award, she'd win it. Heck, even the arrogant, powerful warlocks were afraid of her.

She leaned over and snatched a grape. "I'm hoping you never meet my mother. Remember? Complicated. Extremely complicated."

"I want grape. I want grape." Tom gave Michaela the round piece of fruit.

She popped it in her mouth. "Don't forget to chew," Tom gently instructed. She obliged him, biting down on the grape and slowly chewing.

He looked back over at Wednesday. "I want to meet her."

Wednesday chuckled. "I don't think so."

"But if she's your mother, she can't be so awful."

"Yes, she can."

Tom laughed and raised his eyebrows. "Come on, she can't be that bad."

"Let's just say, she makes your mom's meddling looking angelic."

"That bad? Honestly?" He looked so horrified she burst into giggles.

"My mother is high maintenance, self-absorbed, and unreasonable when it comes to her daughters."

"You have sisters?" he asked, tilting back his head. He hurled another juicy grape toward his mouth.

"I have two. Monday and Tuesday."

Tom lowered his head, and a grape smacked him on the cheek. It fell onto the blanket and rolled in Michaela's direction. She happily picked it up and placed it in her mouth.

"Chew," he reminded her. She smiled, grape juices spilling out the sides of her cheeks. Tom laughed. "You're kidding me about the names, aren't you?"

Wednesday held up three fingers. "Scout's honor," she said, grinning from ear to ear.

"Please don't be offended, because I rather like your name, but the days of the week? There are a billion names out there. Didn't she ever think of reading a baby name book or something?"

"Do you promise not to laugh?"

He crossed his heart with his fingers.

"My mom's name is Sunday."

"No way!"

Wednesday nodded. "And my brother's name is Friday."

Tom's brow furrowed. "Monday, Tuesday, Wednesday. What happened to Thursday?"

"I guess she didn't think it was a very good boy name."

"Okay, so what's your dad's name?"

"Jacob."

Tom hooted with laughter and slapped his thigh with his hand. "Unbelievable. You truly are unique, Wednesday Green."

"Everybody is unique in his or her own way," she told him softly.

"Grape!" shouted Michaela eagerly.

Tom handed her another. "Chew slowly."

"Better call the girls in for lunch." Wednesday lifted the container of fried chicken from the basket. "We wouldn't want to keep you longer than necessary. I'm sure they need you back at the hospital as soon as possible."

"I have no desire to go back to the hospital," he admitted.

Her eyes caught his. "Oh?"

"None whatsoever. Besides, it's meeting day, back to back, the entire day."

Her heart fluttered. His eyes were warm, so very warm. She pushed a strand of hair off her face, curling it behind her ear. "I'm glad."

"I'm glad you're glad."

"Should I get the girls?" she asked.

He shook his head. "Jenna. Tamra. Time for lunch," he yelled over his shoulder, not taking his eyes off Wednesday.

It was hard to remain oblivious to his heated gaze. She tried to ignore her feeling for him, an extraordinarily difficult undertaking, considering he was all she thought about. She popped open a container lid and starting portioning out the fried chicken onto plastic plates and focused on their psychedelic blue and green designed patterns.

Jenna and Tamra ran to them, both red in the cheeks and breathless from physical exertion. Wednesday smiled at the girls. Playing on the monkey bars and jungle gym was not a task for the weak.

"Having fun, Daddy?" Jenna asked.

"Lots," Tom responded.

"Goody." Jenna hugged him hard and kissed his forehead. "You should have more fun, Daddy."

He patted her back and kissed the top of her head. "Thanks, baby."

"You having fun, Wednesday?"

"Very much. Thank you, Tamra."

Jenna and Tamra exchanged happy looks before taking a seat on the picnic blanket.

Wednesday handed Tom a plate loaded with chicken.

"Thanks. Mmmm. It smells delicious."

"An old family recipe."

"From Sunday?"

Wednesday shook her head. "Nope. Great-Grandma Dorcus."

Tom wrinkled his nose. "Ugh. Now that's some name."

"You've got that right."

Tom's foolish grin made Wednesday's heart light. She felt like a schoolgirl experiencing her first crush.

"So, I gotta ask," Tom took a bite of a chicken leg, "are you going to name your kids days of the week."

"Don't be silly."

"Well, I thought since it is a family tradition and all."

"Well, I'm not a big fan of Saturday. That leaves Thursday. I don't particularly care for that either.

"Well, I guess you could use the names of months." He winked at her and swung the bird leg in the air. "This is damn good."

"Damn!" Michaela whooped.

A guilty flush colored Tom's cheeks. "Don't say that," he scolded in his gentle but firm daddy voice.

"But you said it," Jenna pointed out in her very adult voice.

He looked adorable, hunky, and kissable to Wednesday. Discomfort agreed with him. Wednesday leaned back against the tree, interested to see how Tom squirmed his way out of this one. He looked over at her for help, but she shrugged and smiled, munching on an apple.

"But…I shouldn't have. Sometimes I say things I shouldn't."

"Should we spank you now?" inquired Tamra, a milk moustache decorating her upper lip. "You did something bad."

"I'm sorry," Tom said, looking sheepish. "It won't happen again."

"Damn!" Michaela slapped her hands over her mouth and giggled.

"No. Don't say that word again, Michaela."

Wednesday pressed the apple against her lips, covering a smile, as Tom's youngest daughter looked at him with big blue eyes. She blinked her long lashes several times before deciding to bellow out a refrain of the forbidden word.

"A little help from the nanny would be appreciated about now."

Wednesday waved him away. "I think you have this one under control." She zealously bit into the apple.

Tom's glare indicated he was far from it.

For the next few minutes Wednesday watched Tom patiently try to explain to his three inquisitive daughters why that particular word was bad to say.

Michaela occasionally beeped a cheerful refrain between grape munching, but soon turned her attention to a nearby puppy, as any healthy three-year-old would do. A puppy was so much more interesting than bleating out a word she didn't even understand.

"You're a big help," Tom mumbled.

"Thanks. I try to be." She couldn't help chuckling.

They ate the rest of the picnic in amiable silence, placing their full attention on the chattering girls and giving responses to their endless questions.

Wednesday thought it was a very pleasant way to spend the afternoon. The weather was sunny and warm, the food excellent. Grandma's prize winning fried chicken recipe was irresistible. But it was the company making it so perfect.

She wanted Tom to stay. Couldn't he play hooky from work? Lots of people did. But then, not everyone had such an important job. Tom saved lives. He made a difference to so many people.

And yet, his daughters needed him. The wide smiles plastered on their faces told the world how much they loved him, and how ecstatic they were to have him with them for an afternoon rendezvous in the park.

Can't you see how much they need you? Before

you know it you'll be walking them down the aisle, and you'll wonder what happened to those cute kids who used to look at you with such adoration.

Lecturing Tom wouldn't change his mind about the amount of time he spent at his work. Wednesday knew he didn't think very highly of those who tried to advise him about how to run his life. She hadn't forgotten how his eyes turned cold when she tried to meddle. Now that she'd see this version, she preferred the joking, smiling Tom.

But making his children happy was her job. And they'd be truly happy if Tom recognized how much his dedication to work affected his little family in a very negative way. She needed to keep prodding him, needed to be tougher, needed to keep reminding him. The joy of three little girls depended on her.

"I want to swing," Jenna pronounced in her usual bossy way.

"Me too," Tamra chimed in.

"Me!" shouted Michaela through a mouthful of potato salad. She looked up with adoration at her father. "Will you push me?"

Tom took her hand in his and jumped to his feet. "Absolutely."

"Have fun."

"Aren't you coming?"

Wednesday tucked another loose curl behind her ear. "Well, someone has to clean up this mess."

Tom surveyed the remains of the picnic. "It can wait. I'm guessing you're a swinger."

She cocked her head and arched one eyebrow. "You think so?"

"Yep," he said.

"I do enjoy a good swing."

"You go first," Tamra said, pulling Wednesday to her feet.

"Daddy can push you," suggested Jenna, trying to be helpful.

"I think I can handle it."

"No," Tom said moving to Wednesday's side, "I insist. I'm quite a good pusher."

"He is," Tamra and Jenna shouted simultaneously. They ran off toward the swing set. Michaela waddled after them.

"Well, if you insist."

"Most definitely."

He offered her his arm. She looped hers through his.

"It's been awhile," she admitted as they walked.

"Awhile since you swung, or awhile since you *swung*?" he asked, his grin wicked and charming.

"Dr. Anderson! I'm appalled!"

"Really?" He wiggled dark eyebrows at her.

He was flirting with her most outrageously. Wednesday loved it.

She sat in the swing, flipped off her flip-flops and dragged bare toes through the pebbles beneath it. She curled her fingers around the chains, smooth from lots of use.

"Okay, I'm ready."

"Don't be scared," said Michaela.

Wednesday smiled. "I'm not scared."

"I is scared of swings," Michaela stated, her eyes huge and blue, round as buttons, and filled with fright.

"She fell," Jenna said with a giggle.

"I don't think that's very funny," Tom scolded gently. "She could've been hurt."

Jenna's giggles stopped. She dropped her head and dragged her foot through the pebbled sand. "Sorry, Daddy."

Wednesday smiled at Michaela. "But you said you wanted to swing, Michaela honey."

"She always does, but then she gets scared," Jenna piped.

"Jenna, that's enough." Tom's voice was firm.

"What happened to her?" Wednesday asked.

"She was riding on a babysitter's lap, and she slipped and fell."

"Thank goodness she didn't get hurt."

"Yes," Tom said. He smiled at Michaela. "But unfortunately she's been terrified of swings since."

"Michaela, watch me and see how fun it is."

Michaela shook her head. "Swings no fun."

"They can be," Wednesday encouraged. "Watch me, and you'll see how much fun it is."

"Okay," Michaela mumbled with reluctance.

"Give me a push," Wednesday instructed Tom.

"If you insist." He did, gently but firmly.

Wednesday took off for the sky, long legs stretched out in front. She wiggled her toes and laughed when the ten digits brushed the silken leaves of the tree above. Each time she descended, she enjoyed the feel of Tom's hands moving across her lower back as he gave her another push. She heard the girls giggle.

"I'm flying," she called as she made a graceful arc into the air.

The girls clapped. Even Michaela smiled.

It was marvelous fun, but the best part about swinging was the touch of Tom's long fingers on her back. The heat of his skin leaked through the thin fabric of her summer clothing. A few times his hand made contact with bare skin.

It was a simple pleasure, but one Wednesday knew she would never forget.

Chapter Eight

A week later, Wednesday contemplated a career change.

Jenna complained of boredom. She followed Wednesday around the entire morning whining about having nothing to do. Tamra somehow managed to capture Inky and Jazz, locking them in the dryer. The two cats meowed angrily and disappeared for the rest of the day after Wednesday found them and finally released them. Thank goodness the little girl hadn't turned the dryer on. And Michaela had also stuffed the downstairs toilet with an abundance of toilet paper, causing an overflowing mess. The smell greeted Wednesday along with a jubilant three-year-old who couldn't stop smiling.

When Jenna complained for what seemed like the hundredth time, Wednesday lost her cool. "Stop it. I don't want to hear another word out of you about how bored you are. Today we need to stick around the house. I've got house stuff to do."

Jenna stomped her foot. "I want to go to the pool."

Wednesday rolled her eyes. "We're going to the zoo this weekend. I think we can stay home today."

Jenna scowled.

"That look is not becoming," admonished Wednesday, helping Michaela into a fresh pair of clothes.

The scowl deepened.

Wednesday sighed in defeat. "After I clean up the bathroom, we'll do something fun."

A smile replaced the scowl. “Really?”

“Yep. But, I need you to do me a favor first.” Wednesday secured Michaela’s curls away from her baby face with two butterfly barrettes. “You need to take care of your sisters.”

“What are we going to do?” Jenna asked.

Wednesday smiled at the excitement in Jenna’s eyes.

I think I’ve entertained them too much. They’re spoiled.

“I don’t know yet, but I’ll think of something before I’m finished cleaning.” Wednesday brushed a tender kiss against Michaela’s cheek. “There. Finished. I’ll have to lock the bathroom doors to keep you out of mischief.”

Jenna grabbed Michaela’s hand, and they left the room. A moment later, she stuck her head back in. “Can Tamra play?”

Tamra was in time-out after the cat fiasco. The five-year-old sat in the corner of the kitchen on an old chair facing the wall. She wasn’t at all happy about her punishment and had voiced this opinion quite regularly for the last hour.

Wednesday felt weary. “I guess so.”

Jenna popped her head back out the door and hurried down the hall.

Sitting back on her heels, Wednesday surveyed the bathroom disaster from the safety of the hallway. Masses of wet paper filled the white porcelain toilet, hung over the sides, and draped across the floor. An inch of gray water flooded the room, seeping out into the hall. Bright blue, yellow, and pink towels scattered across the floor, a useless attempt to soak up the mess.

She groaned, wishing to be on a beach soaking in the sun and sipping margaritas. She didn’t feel much like cleaning, at least not in the mortal way. She glanced down the hallway, making sure the girls were nowhere around, and then she snapped her fingers together. The water evaporated, the toilet paper disappeared, and the towels cleaned and dried themselves, perfectly folding onto shelves in the small bathroom closet. The room, tropical in theme, sparkled brightly as if it had just been cleaned thoroughly.

Cleaning up messes was a lot easier when one had a little magic in her pocket.

Satisfied, Wednesday slapped her hands together, stood up, and walked the few feet to the family room.

"I see you found something to do."

Jenna nodded. All three girls colored, a rainbow of Crayola crayons spread out between them.

Wednesday flopped down on the couch.

"Did you clean the bathroom?" asked Jenna, her brow wrinkled in suspicion.

"In record time."

"That was fast."

"Super-duper," Wednesday agreed. "So, are you still bored?"

Jenna leaned back in her chair and nodded. "Coloring is fun, but we do it all the time."

"It feeds the imagination."

Jenna looked at her quizzically.

Wednesday pointed to her head and tapped. "All the creativity that lives in here."

"Oh, that," she mumbled, chewing her lower lip.

"I guess I don't have to think of something to entertain you after all."

"You promised," crowed Jenna.

"Did I?"

The seven-year-old looked perplexed for a moment. "No, I guess you didn't promise."

"I've got some ideas." Wednesday picked up a magazine. "But you look happy at the moment."

Jenna grumbled. She picked up a young reader

volume of Lewis Carroll's *Alice's Adventures in Wonderland and Through the Looking Glass.*

"I color," pronounced Michaela with pride as she pointed to her paper.

Wednesday complimented her profusely on her coloring ability. Strawberry Shortcake had never looked so sick. Michaela chose to color her pale blue, and she didn't understand the concept of staying within the lines, yet.

While the girls entertained themselves with coloring outside the lines—she knew the activity wouldn't last long—Wednesday curled up on the couch and flipped on the TV. An old black-and-white episode of *Bewitched* was on. She liked the 60s series, although her mother despised it. Sunday always thought Samantha Stephens was an idiot for marrying a mortal, especially one as closed-minded at Darrin. Sunday did enjoy Endora, but that was it. Needless to say, Sunday was far from delighted when Tuesday announced she was marrying a mortal and an advertising executive at that.

"Is Daddy coming?" asked Tamra hopefully.

It seemed she'd recovered from her exile to the corner. She was willing to forgive Wednesday for such an evil punishment and, and once again, speak to her.

"Nope. Your father's in surgery today. He'll be home tonight."

"For dinner?" Jenna inquired.

"Yep."

"Can we have pizza?" Tamra asked.

"Pizza!" giggled Michaela tossing her blue crayon on the floor, and she picked up the color orange.

"Pizza it is," Wednesday said.

It was the easiest meal. All she had to do was pick up the phone, order it, and a tasty sphere of scrumptious food would be delivered. Nothing was quicker or simpler than that. Except for maybe using her magic.

The girls weren't alone in their hope Tom would join them for a meal. Wednesday missed him, even more so after they'd spent such a marvelous time at the park. She remembered the tenderness of his smile and the sparkling humor in his eyes.

He looked so damn good in a pair of faded jeans and a T-shirt; she hadn't been able to take her eyes off him. They suited him much better than the stuffy suit and tie. Hmm, she wondered how he looked in scrubs. Heat rose in her cheeks. She still felt the warm imprint of his hands on her back and smiled, remembering rising higher and higher in the swing, so high her bare toes touched the branches of a tall oak tree.

Their lunch together had been so normal. The girls giggled often, Tom laughed, and Wednesday felt part of a family. The feeling of belonging to such a family brought a lump to her throat and tears to her eyes.

Her family hadn't ever been close. They happened to be spread out all around the world. Oh, they'd come running if she ever needed them, arriving faster than she could say hocus-pocus, but they seldom managed to get together.

Family gatherings were practically non-existent. Sunday flittered about the world, Monday made her home in the Riviera, Friday never cared to stay in one place too long, and Tuesday was busy with her family, a doting husband and four kids, two sons and two daughters.

Wednesday wanted a family of her very own. She longed for stability, children, a home, and to love and be loved. She didn't think it was a lot to ask, but it had been impossible to find until now.

Her heart skipped a beat.

I love them. I love him. What am I going to do?

Wednesday looked over at the girls. They busily scribbled away, giving life to the characters decorating the coloring book pages.

Her heart ached. How was she going to leave them when the time came? How could she turn her back on them and walk out as if they didn't matter to her? She couldn't do it. She wouldn't leave them. They meant too much to her.

Wednesday knew that one day soon she'd have to leave Tom and his girls. It was impossible for her to stay; this was only a job and a temporary one at that. She didn't want to face it. Once her job was completed, she'd have to leave. Those were the rules.

Besides, how could she ever tell Tom she loved him? They'd shared a few kisses, body-tingling sexy kisses, but he'd never spoken of love, and she wasn't about to bring it up. She wasn't ready to face having her heart shattered; she didn't know if he loved her or not was better.

The intensity in the kisses they'd shared had been so passionate and full of such sweet tenderness. she believed he had to care for her a little bit.

Maybe he even loved her, but that still wouldn't make things work between them. There was a much bigger problem at stake than her just being the nanny. She was a witch with magical powers and a life expectancy of, well, nearly forever, certainly longer than Tom and the girls. How would Tom react to that?

"I'm bored again," Jenna announced, closing the Lewis Carroll book. "I don't want to read or color."

And I want to think about Tom.

"Okay, have any ideas?" Wednesday turned off the TV and gave her full attention to Jenna.

"That's your job."

Wednesday fought the urge to stick out her tongue at the bossy seven-year-old. She adored Jenna, but sometimes the little girl pushed all her irritation buttons.

"We could make cookies."

"No."

"How about a game?"

"No." Jenna shook her head.

"A movie?" Wednesday placed an elbow on the arm of the couch and leaned her cheek against the palm of her right hand.

"No." The seven-year-old sat up, wrapping slim arms around knobby knees.

"We could go to the park," Wednesday suggested.

Jenna wrinkled her nose. "No."

"Maybe all three of you need a nap."

"No!" they screamed in unison.

"How about croquet?"

"What's that?" Jenna asked.

"A game."

"I told you I didn't want to play any game." She crossed her arms in front of her. Anger glowed from her eyes.

"Well, you play this game outside. Don't you remember reading about it in your book?"

Jenna shook her head.

"Well, you haven't gotten to that part yet," Wednesday said gently.

"Outside! Go outside!" chimed Michaela, seemingly very happy with the idea.

"How do you play?" Jenna inquired.

Wednesday jumped off the couch. "Can you grab me your Alice book?"

Jenna looked at her oddly, but obeyed.

Wednesday noticed another classic underneath *Alice's Adventures in Wonderland*. "Oh, and bring *Peter Pan and Wendy* too."

"A game with books?" Jenna asked. She clutched the hardcover picture books to her chest.

"You'll see."

Wednesday picked up Michaela and beckoned the other two girls to follow her out the sliding patio doors to the flagstone patio. They did, as curious as two cats. The sweeping green lawn spread out before them, enclosed by a high brick wall decorated with an abundance of flowers, bushes and trees.

Wednesday spread the books flat on the stone patio, waved her hands across the pages, and summoned forth the nanny sheepdog from *Peter Pan*.

Jenna gasped. Tamra's eyes grew as huge as saucers.

Wednesday held a finger to her lips. "This is a secret. Promise not to tell?"

They nodded, dumbfounded by the wagging dog before them.

"You watch her," Wednesday instructed the dog, pointing to Michaela.

The massive sheepdog nodded her head and licked Michaela's glowing face. The toddler fell over in a spasm of giggles.

"Now for your entertainment." Wednesday winked at Jenna and Tamra. She flicked her fingers over Lewis Carroll book and whispered a few enchanting words.

Out popped an assortment of characters from the beloved story, including an astonished Alice, an alarmed White Rabbit, and a fuming Queen of Hearts.

"Hello."

"WHO ARE YOU?" demanded the Queen.

"I'm Wednesday, Your Majesty." Wednesday remembered to curtsy. The Queen of Hearts hated it when subjects didn't pay her the respect due her station.

"Wednesday who?"

"That's not important."

The queen's black eyes glared at Wednesday. "I

say it is."

The White Rabbit's whiskers twitched. He hopped from foot to foot, nervous as usual.

"How do you do, Miss Wednesday," said Alice, lowering her petite body into a respectful curtsy.

"Wow!" cried out Jenna.

Tamra was too enthralled to say a word. She stared in open-mouthed wonder.

"I believe you were about to play a game of croquet," said Wednesday.

"Yes. We're late," muttered the White Rabbit, holding up his oversized pocket watch for everyone to see.

"You aren't late," Wednesday soothed. She'd dealt with these characters before. It had always been her favorite way to entertain her nieces and nephews. She'd learned the trick in Entertaining Children 101.

The White Rabbit looked about him, replacing the golden watch into the pocket of his vest. "But these aren't the Queen's gardens."

Wednesday snapped her fingers and the royal croquet set from Wonderland, complete with colorful flamingos and pudgy hedgehogs, appeared on the green lawn.

"Splendid," said the Queen, with a wide smile.

"Have a good time," Wednesday said. She walked back toward the house, paused, and added, "And no one loses their heads today."

The Queen huffed. Alice smiled and introduced herself to Jenna, Tamra, and Michaela. The White Rabbit removed the watch from his pocket and held it to his ear. He shook it and then listened to it again. Soon, he was jumping around and cursing the absent March Hare for destroying his favorite pocket watch.

Wednesday chuckled as she stepped into the family room. The flamboyant creatures from

Wonderland always seemed to entertain. And the sheepdog from *Peter Pan* was the best babysitter around, even sharing her child rearing knowledge as a guest lecturer at Magical Nanny University.

Now, she could get some housework done.

Tom really should hire a housekeeper. He could afford it.

She groaned when the phone rang. She thought about letting the answering machine get it, but changed her mind. It might be Tom. And she never passed up the chance to talk to him.

It was Tom.

"What's up?" he asked.

"Not much."

"Munchkins giving you a bad time?"

"Never. Good as gold." She sank into an overstuffed chair and dangled her legs over one arm. "What's up with you?"

She could hear his shrug through the phone.

"I just wanted to see how things were."

"Tom, I've been here for awhile now. Don't you trust me yet?"

A hedgehog croquet ball rolled into the family room. Wednesday watched as a stressed White Rabbit hurried in and smacked it with the beak of a squawking flamingo croquet mallet.

Wednesday covered her eyes and sank further into the comfy chair. She hoped Tom hadn't heard that.

He had. "What was that?"

Her heart sank.

"Must be a bird or something. I'm in the backyard."

She hated lying to him.

The White Rabbit waved before vanishing outside.

But how could she tell him the truth. How would Dr. Tom Anderson, renowned surgeon, react to finding out the Queen of Hearts, Alice and the White Rabbit played a game of croquet in his backyard, with his children?

He most likely wouldn't believe a word of it.

"Oh" Tom paused "I wanted to tell you how much I enjoyed yesterday."

She smiled into the phone. "I had a good time, too."

"I was thinking, maybe, I can join you and the kids at the zoo this Saturday."

Wednesday straightened up in the chair. "That would be great. The girls would love it and so would I."

He cleared his throat.

She smiled. He sounded nervous.

"I feel as if I talk to you more over the phone than face to face."

"Yeah, me too," she agreed. "That's what happens when you work as much as you do."

"I can never say no," he admitted. "I end up doing more than just surgeries. I've lost count of how many committees I'm on, always writing articles for medical journals, and filling in for co-workers every chance I get. You think I need to stop?"

"Yes," she replied simply. "Your profession is important, Tom, and I admire what you do, but your little girls need you."

"Yeah," he said softly.

"Yeah," she repeated just as softly.

She heard the softness of his breath on the other end of the phone. She wanted to help him find a balance between his work and family, but she didn't know how.

"I'll see you tonight."

She leaned her cheek against the couch's flowered upholstery. "I'm looking forward to it."

"Can I bring anything home for dinner?"

"We planned on pizza." She traced the pattern of

a rose with one pointer finger.

"I'll swing by and pick it up on the way home."

"Thanks."

"Large? Canadian bacon? Pineapple?"

"Perfect." She loved the sound of his voice.

"See you later."

"Later, Tom."

She laid the phone in its cradle. Elation swelled her heart. She was making progress with him. She clasped her hands together and tears filled her eyes. She'd be successful at her first job, and Jenna, Tamra and Michaela would have their father back. And…he would have them. Then…

I will have to leave.

Her heart plummeted. She never wanted to leave.

A polite cough caused Wednesday to turn her head.

Alice curtsied politely.

"Is something wrong?" Wednesday asked.

The fictional girl's smile was bright and cheery. "Not at all, Miss Wednesday. We are having a wonderful time."

"But?"

"It is time for tea."

Wednesday glanced at the clock on the mantle of the fireplace. It chimed two o'clock.

"And tea shall be served," she said, hopping up from the couch.

"Oh, that is marvelous! I shall go and tell the White Rabbit and the Queen, immediately!" cried Alice, before skipping out of the room.

Wednesday supposed the White Rabbit would have a heart attack if things were not done on time.

"After tea, you're all going back in the book," Wednesday muttered.

She summoned up a tea tray filled with a dainty teapot, cups, saucers, and delicious treats direct from her uncle's London restaurant.

Two hours later, she popped the characters back into the book. Jenna and Tamra couldn't stop gushing about the croquet game and the tea party following. They seemed to have forgotten it was supposed to be a secret. Wednesday didn't want to make them forget the thrilling day, but she also didn't want Tom thinking his daughters had lost their minds.

When she warned them again to not go telling people about the croquet match and tea party, they agreed, but Wednesday wondered if they would slip. She suspected they'd forget and mention it. Somehow, she doubted this would stay a secret.

Exhausted Michaela fell asleep, sprawled out on her belly in the middle of the family room floor, her old teddy bear folded against her body, the top of his floppy head tucked under her chin. Inky and Jazz were curled up with her. Jazz snuggled blissfully near her head, his nose touching her forehead, while Inky purred happily across her legs. The two cats tolerated Jenna and ignored Tamra. Who could blame them since she'd put them in the dryer? But, they adored Michaela.

Wednesday finally managed to convince the two girls to keep the croquet game quiet, but only after promising to invite the crazy entourage back for a tea party next week. This time, Jenna wanted the Hatter, the March Hare, and the Cheshire Cat to attend. The Cheshire Cat was her absolute favorite, and she wanted to see him make parts of his body disappear.

After solving that dilemma, Wednesday instructed the girls to lie down and close their eyes until Tom came home. They weren't thrilled about a short nap, but they agreed because they didn't want Wednesday to decide against another Wonderland party.

Wednesday finally got a chance to clean the house when the two girls fell asleep on the couch.

****

Tom was more than a little shocked when he opened the front door and found a vacuum zooming past all by itself.

The large pizza with Canadian bacon, pineapple, and extra cheese nearly slipped to the floor. He didn't know much about vacuums, but he was pretty positive that even self-propelled ones weren't supposed to do that.

When he saw the mop waltzing in the middle of the kitchen, he shouted out Wednesday's name, dropped the box of pizza on the table, and tried unsuccessfully to grab the container of cheesy breadsticks. The box flattened against the tiled floor and the breadsticks rolled out.

The mop squeezed itself into a bucket and continued its dance.

Tom watched the mop with fascination and yelped when the vacuum zipped by unaided by a human hand or by electricity.

"Oh, my!"

Tom looked up from the mop and vacuum. Wednesday stood in the doorway, looking quite domestic in a long flowered skirt, blue blouse, and white apron, her long hair wrapped in a loose knot at the back of her neck. Her barefoot exposed ten toes painted with pink nail polish, peaking out from underneath the hem of her long skirt. Tom had never thought he was a foot guy, but then he'd never seen such attractive feet before. Hers took him by surprise—long and narrow, high arched, soft soles, and curved heels, dainty toes. He stopped himself before he asked if she enjoyed foot massages. That would have been too personal a question to ask his nanny.

She looked horrified to find him standing in the

kitchen.

"Ummm, Wednesday, do you think you can explain this?" he asked, gesturing to the twirling mop.

She grabbed for the vacuum. "You're home early."

"Well?" he prodded.

He liked finding her standing in his kitchen, even with a berserk vacuum dodging her outstretched hand. Coming home to her every day would be like a little piece of heaven on earth.

Wednesday managed to grasp the vacuum with one hand and winked. The vacuum immediately went silent. She winked again and the mop fell to the floor.

"A problem with your eye?" he asked.

She blushed.

Tom thought the pink in her cheeks looked rather becoming.

"An eyelash," she said.

Tom thought he detected a bit of nervousness in her voice. He'd be interested in hearing how she explained her way out of this one. She was an odd one, but he rather liked her. Actually, he kind of liked her a whole lot. Her oddities made her unique and interesting, and the combination was amazingly attractive.

"So" he sat down and placed his arms across his chest "explain yourself."

Her blush intensified. She shifted her weight from one foot to the other. She reminded him of a kid with her hand caught in the cookie jar.

"Am I to believe a mop and a vacuum clean magically all by themselves?"

She released the vacuum. It stayed in place, not moving an inch. "I'm a practicing magician."

Her smile made two dimples form high in her cheeks. Now, why hadn't he noticed those before?

Every time he looked at her he discovered something new.

"A magician?"

She nodded. "Yes, I'm an amateur, but I rather enjoy it."

Tom let loose an impressed whistle. "I wouldn't call that too amateurish. You're rather remarkable."

With a wave of her arms, she made a quick bow in his direction. "Thank you."

He didn't know if he believed her explanation or not, but then what else could it be?

"I didn't know I hired a regular Houdini."

She shrugged. "Now, you know. I'm kind of embarrassed about it, actually."

"Why? I think you could start your own professional act. It convinced me."

She grinned crookedly.

"Are you going to share your secret?"

"Absolutely not. Magician's never share the secret behind their tricks."

"Yes, but I'm quite interested in how you managed to make a vacuum work without being plugged in. I saw the cord dangling behind it, not plugged into any socket, and I watched a mop clean the floor and wring itself out, all by itself."

"You'll just have to be curious. It's okay to not know all the answers, Tom. I'll never confess my secrets."

"Well, you convinced me the impossible was happening."

Wednesday grinned. "Good."

"Hungry?" he asked.

She nodded. "Famished."

"Well, I've got pizza."

She laughed, looking at the floor. "Minus the breadsticks."

He grimaced, looking at Tamra's favorite appetizers scattered in all directions over the kitchen floor.

"I'll get the dustpan and broom."

"Oh, can't you just twitch a nose or something and make them disappear?" he joked.

Was it his imagination or did she seem to pale considerably? Her smile did disappear rather abruptly.

"That's not funny," she whispered.

"I thought it was." Tom turned his attention to gathering plates, napkins, silverware, and cans of pop from the refrigerator.

Wednesday quickly swept up the breadsticks and discarded the cheesy pieces in the wastebasket under the sink.

Jenna raced into the room. "Daddy! Daddy! We had the best day!"

Tom ruffled her hair. "Tell me about it."

And Jenna proceeded to gush about how she'd spent the day playing croquet and having tea with Alice, the White Rabbit, and the Queen of Hearts.

Tom chuckled at her fantastical tale. "Where were the Hatter and March Hare?" he asked.

"Not there," said Jenna. "But next time. Wednesday promised."

"You bring out the imagination in my children, Wednesday Green."

"Is that a good or bad thing?" she asked.

"Oh, it's a very good thing."

Jenna tugged on his arm. "Daddy, I wasn't supposed to say anything about the tea party." She looked over at Wednesday her smile shy. Tom noticed she looked just a little bit guilty.

"That's okay, Jenna." Wednesday ruffled the girl's curls. "Secrets are never a good thing anyway."

Tom's hand brushed Wednesday's as he took the broom and dustpan. She jumped slightly at his touch. A spark of heat erupted up his arm at their touch, his fingers lingered for a moment against hers.

"Perhaps next time, I can join the tea party," he whispered.

"That would be fun. I'd love to have you at our tea party," said Jenna.

He stared deep into Wednesday's eyes. "What do you say?"

"Oh, I don't think you'd like it," Wednesday said with a smile. "You don't seem like a tea party type of guy."

"I think I may enjoy a tea party with you."

"I'm hungry, Daddy."

"Let's eat," said Wednesday, turning away.

It took all his will power to step away from her. It was the last thing he wanted to do. He'd rather have Wednesday Green than pizza any day.

Chapter Nine

Tom had promised to go to the Minnesota Zoo with them, but Wednesday didn't believe he would until Saturday morning when he loaded up the kids and her into the nanny mobile, as he called the family SUV.

Wednesday was positive something would prevent him from going to the zoo, mainly Anjelica, who'd called his cell phone twenty times in the past two hours. She obviously wasn't pleased he was spending the entire day away from her.

In spite of her feelings, Wednesday listened politely while Tom chatted with Anjelica over the phone nearly the entire way to the city of Apple Valley. He promised her he'd attend some big hospital hoopla that evening and wished her a good day.

Wednesday smirked as she imagined a sputtering, angry Anjelica on the other end. Marketing and public relations guru, Anjelica probably didn't give a hoot if he spent the day with his children, but the idea of him spending the day with a halfway attractive nanny was another story entirely.

She couldn't resist asking how the diva was doing.

"She's a pain," Tom admitted, folding his phone and setting it on the dashboard.

Wednesday looked out the window. "I won't argue there."

"She has her good points."

Wednesday didn't believe it. Most people did,

but she found it impossible to believe Anjelica had a redeeming bone in her size two body.

"Really?" she asked, turning to look at him. "And what might those be?"

Tom's brow creased in concentration. "Well, she's good looking."

"Please," Wednesday waved her hand in the air, "you aren't that superficial."

"You don't like her."

"Am I that obvious?" she asked innocently.

"I don't think she's too fond of you, either."

Wednesday scrunched up her face. "I'm not surprised. She wasn't overly warm to me the night of the dinner."

"Yeah, I noticed." He leaned forward to turn off the radio. "She barely thanked you for such an incredible meal. I still don't know how you did it."

"Just call me Super Nanny."

He grinned. "Yes, that's what you are, Miss Wednesday Green. I don't know what we did without you."

"Neither do I, Dr. Anderson. You needed me badly."

"Badly," he agreed. His eyes twinkled.

"We're here!" Jenna squealed.

"Yippy!" Tamra shouted.

Michaela clapped her hands repeatedly and hugged her teddy bear.

"I've never been to the Minnesota Zoo," Wednesday said.

"Oh, you'll love it," Tom assured as he parked the car in the Toucan Parking Lot. "It's a nice zoo. Haven't been here in a few years, now though. Mary loved to take the kids up here. I think they went once a month during the summer."

"An animal lover?" Wednesday unlocked the car door and pushed it open.

"A big animal lover," he said as she stepped from

the car.

She turned back, holding the door in her hand. "But you don't have any animals now."

"I happen to have two cats," Tom corrected with a lazy smile.

"I hope they aren't too much trouble."

Tom placed his keys and phone in the pocket of his khaki pants. "Not at all. I'm learning to like them. I never was a cat lover, but they're quite comical. I've had a few good laughs watching their antics. They have their good points."

"Just like Anjelica?" Wednesday asked sweetly. She just couldn't resist the comparison.

Green eyes sparkled with vibrant warmth. "I guess so."

Wednesday closed the passenger door and opened the back door. "I know one thing Anjelica has in common with cats," she said.

Tom turned in his seat. "What's that?"

Wednesday unhooked Michaela from her car seat, lifting her up and securing the three-year-old at the hip. "Claws," she replied.

Tom chuckled. "I guess I can't argue with that. She's tenacious." He got out of the car, closed his driver's door, and walked to the back of the vehicle. He flung open the back hatch and pulled out the stroller.

Wednesday walked around the car while Michaela bubbled excitedly in her arms and then Tom helped Wednesday secure Michaela in the stroller.

Wednesday's skin tingled where his hand brushed hers. She noticed his long fingers for the first time and admired how elegant his hands were. He had beautiful, strong hands—life-saving, skilled surgeon's hands. The tingling spread and her thoughts strayed.

How skilled are those hands in bed?

She felt her face flame so brightly; she turned away, shielding her burning face with the curtain of her hair. Shame on her—such wicked thoughts about her employer! Oh, heavens, she shouldn't have kissed him in the garden or in the family room or in the kitchen. She just shouldn't have kissed him! She couldn't stop thinking about being close to him—plastered against him. He was constantly on her mind, every second, of every minute, of every hour, of every day.

Jenna clamored down from the SUV dressed in a red and white polka-dot shirt, pastel striped shorts, and green sandals. She didn't care one bit she was rather mismatched. She insisted on picking out her own clothes, and so, Wednesday let her. Wednesday knew when to pick her battles and a matching outfit debate was not one of them.

"Wednesday, we want to see the tigers first," she pronounced with authority.

"I want to see the dolphins first," Tamra cried out in protest, glaring at her big sister. "We don't got to do what you want all the time."

"I'm older," Jenna declared.

"That doesn't mean you always get to decide." Tom patted the top of her head. "How about we let Wednesday choose what we see first?"

The little girls turned their attention to their nanny.

"Dolphins," Tamra encouraged sweetly.

"Tigers," Jenna announced as if there was no way anyone would dare defy her.

"I is hungry," mumbled Michaela forlornly.

Wednesday gave Tom an *I-don't-have-a-clue-what-we-should-see-first* look.

"Do you enjoy flowers?" he asked.

"Immensely," Wednesday said, remembering their kiss amidst the summer flowers near the guest cottage.

"If I remember correctly, there are a variety of orchids along the Tropics Trail."

Wednesday was relieved not have to choose between tigers and dolphins. Someone was bound to be unhappy.

"I'd like to see the orchids," she said.

Jenna stuck out her tongue while Tamra imperiously told Wednesday flowers were boring.

"To the Tropics Trail first," Tom pushed Michaela forward in the stroller, "and then, we'll check out the tigers and dolphins."

"Tigers before dolphins," Jenna said.

Tamra punched her in the arm.

"Ouch!"

"Stop that." Wednesday grabbed Tamra's hand. "We don't hit each other."

"We'll see the dolphins first, because they're closer to the Tropics Trail," Tom said as they approached the entrance.

Loads of kids and parents already flooded in through the zoo's gates.

"Hungry," Michaela whined.

"I don't want to see the dolphins first." Jenna stuck out her lower lip stubbornly.

"We're off to a great start," Tom said.

"Are you having second thoughts?" Wednesday inquired as she searched her straw bag for the plastic bag of Cheerios she'd tossed in.

"They'll be exhausted by noon."

Wednesday almost hoped so. Jenna and Tamra were going to be a handful. She handed Michaela the Cheerios.

"I hope the zoo is ready for us."

Tom slipped his credit card to the attendant at the ticket stand. "Me, too."

"Thanks, but you didn't have to pay my way," Wednesday said.

"Spending the day at the zoo with us isn't the

most relaxing thing to do."

"I wouldn't want to be anywhere else."

He stared into her eyes. "Me neither. I'm happy I decided to come."

Wednesday smiled. She wanted to throw her arms about his neck and lock lips with him, but that was impossible. She was his children's nanny. He was seeing someone else and still mourning his wife. She needed to keep things purely professional. She was a witch; he was a mortal. There were too many obstacles to overcome and there was no point lingering on what could never be.

She enjoyed the Tropics Trail. The exhibit was lush, green, and abundant with flowering orchids of all shapes and colors. The girls exclaimed excitedly over the lemurs, while she paused to read each marker.

"There are over one thousand orchids grown and maintained at the zoo," she read off one of the plaques.

"Did you hear that?" Tom asked his girls.

Michaela hummed softly in the stroller, the bag of Cheerios long emptied, lay in her lap. Jenna and Tamra were up ahead admiring the gibbons.

"I guess they aren't too interested in flowers."

Tom pushed the stroller along the winding path. "Guess not. I probably wasn't too interested in them either at that age."

"And, you are now?"

"Not really. I thought you'd like them."

They passed a vibrant array of burgundy and purple orchids.

"Oh, I do. I like them very much."

And Wednesday truly did. They were beautiful. She sighed happily as they rounded a bend in the path revealing another bunch of the exotic flowers. This was the most perfect day. Tom and the girls were spending much needed time together. And she had his attention.

"I'm assuming roses are your favorite flower."

"Why?" she asked, admiring a particularly flamboyant pink orchid.

"Aren't they every woman's?"

"No, not mine. Roses are beautiful," she said softly, "but my favorite flower is a sunflower."

"That surprises me. I never thought of sunflowers.

"They are so, well, sunny."

"Have you ever seen a field of them?"

"Oh, yes, many times. Nothing compares."

"I don't know about that. There are a few things I can think of that are more lovely."

There was something warm and suggestive in his voice that made her heart flip-flop. She felt his eyes on her and didn't trust herself to look at him. She didn't trust what she'd do if she saw what she thought she'd see in his eyes. Avoiding his gaze, she stopped to read another plaque, this time about the tree kangaroos.

"Can we see the dolphins, now?" Jenna asked.

"I thought you didn't want to see the dolphins."

She scowled. Jenna had perfected the scowl. There was no doubt about that.

Jenna and Tamra ran ahead.

"Ready for dolphins?"

Wednesday nodded, tucking loose tendrils of hair behind her ears. Her leg brushed against his as they exited the rainforest exhibit. Heat emanated up her leg.

"Sorry," she apologized.

"I like having you close," he whispered, taking her hand. His finger caressed the sensitive skin of her palm.

Wednesday shivered. "Please, don't," she pleaded. She looked up at him.

The heavy tropic air encircled them in its

embrace, but the humid heat was nothing compared to the sizzling desire she saw blazing from his eyes.

"Why do I want you so much?" he murmured. He stepped closer. His lips touched the delicate curve of her ear. She shuddered. Her skin flamed.

Does he have any idea how that makes me feel?

"Don't." Even to her own ears her voice was not very convincing.

He kissed her ear again.

"Stop." She turned her head in the opposite direction, avoiding his onslaught of erotic kisses.

"I can't help myself. You're so beautiful."

Wednesday pulled her hand away. "We mustn't. We're just friends. Remember?"

He nodded. His hand dropped to his side. "I guess, but I can't resist you."

She decided to be honest with him. She couldn't resist him, either. She couldn't fight him. She cared too much about him. "You're kind of irresistible too."

He leaned forward again, and Wednesday bolted up the path after Jenna and Tamra. She had to resist him.

She wanted so much more than friendship or a strictly professional relationship. She hungered for him, wanted to be near him always. Her feelings were more than sexual attraction; she knew it. She loved him.

****

For the next five hours Wednesday tried very hard to concentrate on the zoo's exhibits, but it proved next to impossible. The recollection of Tom's lips on her super-sensitive skin made it hard to concentrate on anything else. She'd never spent an entire day alone with him and she'd loved every minute of it. The picnic in the park had been great, but being with him for more than a couple of hours was absolutely fabulous.

The man was amazing to watch with his

children. He was a wonderful father, solving arguments between Jenna and Tamra effortlessly, when she needed magic to make peace between them, and he'd entertained a cranky Michaela by pretending to be some ridiculous bird. She'd needed a real bird, the last time she'd tried to entertain the adorable child.

Because, Wednesday guessed he felt just a wee bit guilty for avoiding them as much as he had, he also spoiled them. In any case, he seemed to be having fun, and money wasn't one of his concerns.

They exited the zoo with a menagerie of souvenirs. Jenna received a stuffed Amur tiger and Tamra exclaimed with delight over a gigantic dolphin kite. Wednesday picked out a wacky looking stuffed monkey for Michaela. The poor kid was so tuckered out that she fell fast asleep in the stroller and missed the expedition to the store. Wednesday was relieved because the munchkin would've wanted everything in the place. Tom bought all three girls an odd assortment of plastic toys, coloring books, educational books, animal-shaped balloons, and a fridge magnet in the shape of a caribou with "Minnesota Zoo" spelled out across the antlers.

On the way back to the car, with the children arguing, souvenirs tumbling, and Michaela snoring, Wednesday started to laugh.

"What's so funny?" Tom asked.

She covered her mouth, unable to stop the cascade of giggles. He looked utterly ridiculous laden down with the girls' toys, and wearing an outlandish hat with large antlers on his head. He made the mistake of letting Jenna and Tamra pick out his zoo token. The two imps selected the crazy hat, the ugliest souvenir in the place. The only good thing about the hat was it had been on sale; he got a whopping great deal on it.

"You're laughing at my hat." His eyes rolled up,

looking at the brim, while adjusting the tiger under his arm. "Are you embarrassed to be seen with me?"

Wednesday leaned over Michaela's stroller and laughed harder. "I feel like we're in a scene from a movie."

"Yeah, I think I know the one," Tom chuckled. A gust of wind blew the three balloons he had tied to his wrist into his face. "The one with Steve Martin and all the kids."

"*Parenthood.*"

"Right. *Parenthood.*"

"It happens to be one of my favorites."

Tom struggled with the balloons.

Wednesday started laughing again. She couldn't help it. He looked so comical standing in the middle of the Toucan Lot with a lopsided antler hat, a huge stuffed tiger, and an array of misbehaving balloons.

"I don't think we need to come back to the zoo for awhile," she laughed.

His eyes twinkled. He tilted his head to one side. "Didn't you have a good time?"

They stopped in front of the SUV. He fumbled to find his keys, spinning in a small circle as he tried to find his pocket. After a few moments of struggling, he pulled them out, waggled them in front of her nose in victory, and unlocked all the doors with one push of a single button.

"This wouldn't be a bad groundhog day. I could definitely relive this one a few more times."

He kissed her cheek, startling her. But his affectionate peck seemed so natural.

"Thanks," he said with a wink, "for making it such a special day for my girls and me."

Wednesday clutched the stroller handles, very afraid her knees might buckle. She didn't know what to say. Instead, she opted to say nothing, knowing she didn't have to say anything at all. The day had been special, for all of them.

They loaded into the car surprisingly fast, and by the time they reached U.S. Hwy 52, the girls were fast asleep.

Wednesday dreaded returning home. She wanted to keep him away from possessive Anjelica. If only she could convince him not to attend Anjelica's shindig.

"They might be too tired to go to the fair tonight," she observed.

The three did look exhausted. Heads lobbed up and down, rolling from side to side. Eyelashes fluttered slightly against rosy cheeks, and all three snored softly.

"Sometimes, I try to plan too many activities," Wednesday sighed.

"They've been spoiled enough today," Tom said. "They'll have to go to the fair next week."

"But it won't be here then. Remember? It finishes at the end of this weekend."

"That's too bad."

Wednesday decided not to think twice about asking him go to the fair. Part of her task included making Dr. Tom Anderson live life a little more fully. Somewhere along the way, he'd forgotten there was more to life than work, no matter how rewarding the work happened to be.

She took a deep breath and dived in, "How about you and I go?"

"It sounds fun, but—"

She wasn't about to back down. He was melting. She knew it. "I'm sure your mom will watch the kids."

"Yeah, she's been talking about the fair for the past few days. She says I need to get out more."

"Well, you do."

"I'm going out tonight."

"Oh, right. With Anjelica." Wednesday played with the zipper on her purse. "You'd have more fun at the fair, and I think your mother meant for you to get away from work. Isn't tonight a work thing?"

"I promised."

"You won't reconsider?" she asked. "I can be a lot of fun." She fluttered her lashes dramatically at him.

He laughed. "I know you're fun. I had a blast with you today and yesterday and every moment I've spent with you since you showed up on my doorstep and demanded the job."

"I did no such thing!" she cried out in self-defense.

"You did so."

"Okay, maybe I did demand—a little," she consented.

"We'll do it some other time."

"What if Anjelica gets sick and cancels?"

Tom snorted. "Anjelica has never been sick a day in her life. She's an exercise and fitness nut."

"But, if she cancelled?"

"I would think about it."

"No guarantees?" she prodded gently.

"None."

"You're no fun at all," she told him.

He ignored her comment. "She isn't going to cancel. Trust me on this. I know Anjelica."

Wednesday smirked. That's what he thought. She may not be able to cure diseases and save lives, but she could use witchcraft to cause a little bit of misery.

His cell rang. He flipped it open, glanced at the number, and caught Wednesday's eye.

"Who is it?" she asked sweetly.

"Anjelica."

"What a coincidence!" she exclaimed.

"Is it?" He eyed her suspiciously.

"Don't act so surprised. I'm sure she's calling to make sure you're on the way home. She'll probably be waiting for us at the door."

Tom answered Anjelica's call.

Wednesday pretended to dig for an item in her purse, but she listened with interest to Tom's side of the conversation.

"What's up? Oh? That's too bad? A flu bug, you say? Sounds nasty. No, I feel fine. Something you ate?"

Wednesday arched her eyebrows as Tom held the phone away from his ear.

"Puking," he explained in a whisper.

Wednesday tried to keep a serious face. "How awful for her. Tell her I hope she feels better. Guess you won't be going to the black tie affair after all."

He gave her an odd look.

"I hope you feel better," Tom soothed. "No. I'm not going without you. I don't have to be there. Others will cover. I think I'll stay home with the kids tonight. Come over there? I don't think so. I don't want to risk bringing anything home to the girls. You stay home and sleep it off. I'll talk to you tomorrow." He snapped his phone shut.

"Sounds bad," commented Wednesday, a little too happily. She pulled out a tube of lip-gloss and a small mirror.

"It is. You didn't hear her. She sounds plain awful."

"And you said she never gets sick." Wednesday held up the mirror in front of her and rolled the tube of gloss on her lips.

"She doesn't. It's rather strange."

Wednesday avoided his suspicious glance. She capped the tube and dropped it and the mirror back into the depths of her oversized bag. "Well, now you can go to the fair with me."

"Didn't you hear what I just said?"

"What did you just say?" she asked innocently.

"That I'm going to stay at home with the girls."

"Them?" Wednesday asked, jutting her thumb

over her shoulder in the direction of the sleeping girls. "You think they're going to be good company tonight. They'll be too tired to be any fun at all."

"I'm not going despite the fact you and my mother seem insistent I go."

"It'll be fun."

He sighed. "I think I've had enough fun for one day."

"No one can have *enough* fun."

He ran his fingers through his hair. "Wednesday, you do make my life lively, but I'm still not going."

"Your loss. I guess I'll have to go by myself."

"Oh, that sounds like fun."

His sarcastic tone caused her to lift her chin.

"I can have fun by myself. I don't need others to entertain me."

"I'll think about it and give you my answer when we get home."

She crossed her arms over her chest. "Well, maybe I don't want you to go after all."

"Oh, I think you do," he chuckled.

She turned and glared out the window.

Thirty minutes later, they pulled into the circular driveway leading up to the house. She'd gotten over her irritation with him and had asked him about attending the fair again. His answer was still a firm "no way." He finally admitted he didn't enjoy fairs. He hated the rides and the food. Heck, he hated the atmosphere in general.

"I can change your mind about that," she insisted. Wednesday happened to love everything about fairs. "I have a soft spot for mini donuts and cheese curds and fluffy pink cotton candy." She also held a special fondness for carousels.

He shook his head. "I'm not going. It's just not my type of thing."

"You should try new things, doctor."

"Come on, drop this," he groaned, "and help me carry the kids inside."

She obliged, cradling Michaela against her chest. Tom followed with Tamra draped over his shoulder and Jenna sleepily holding onto his hand.

To Wednesday's surprise the house blazed with lights.

"What the—?"

Janet Anderson stepped out of the dining room, instantly silencing her son's unfinished question. She smiled and took Michaela from Wednesday.

"Welcome home. How was the zoo?"

"What are you doing here, mother?"

"I thought you might need a babysitter," Janet said. She gave Wednesday a wink.

Jenna greeted her grandma with a tired yawn.

Janet kissed the top of her granddaughter's head and told her milk and cookies awaited in the kitchen. Jenna wandered off, pulling her stuffed tiger behind her. Tamra followed, rubbing her eyes and dragging her stuffed dolphin.

Inky and Jazz started playing with the toys, overjoyed at the prospect of two fake creatures to play with.

"I'm not going. I already told Wednesday I'm not into fairs."

"Too bad. I'm chasing you out. You can't deny your mother a few hours alone with her grandchildren."

"Mother, you see them almost every day," Tom said calmly.

"And I never tire of them." Janet kissed Michaela's forehead.

"It's been a long day," Tom said.

"The fair will rejuvenate you, and you'll be with Wednesday. What can be better than that?"

Tom opened his mouth to respond, but snapped it shut quickly.

"I'm sorry to hear about Anjelica. She called here asking if you were home yet. She sounded terrible."

"Some flu bug," Wednesday said.

"Well, no reason for her illness to affect your fun." Janet patted Tom's cheek. She was treating him like a little boy, and Wednesday found it quite amusing.

He conceded. "Oh, all right." He stared at the ceiling in exasperation. "I can't fight you both."

Chapter Ten

The car ride to the fairgrounds took a whole of ten minutes. The city of Rallington had a population of approximately 90,000, a relatively small city as cities went. It had a small town feel and a person could easily get from one end to the other in fifteen minutes. But it was growing by leaps and bounds. Most of the growth was due to the fact a world famous medical center had made the city its home for over one hundred years.

As they drove through downtown on the way to the grounds, Wednesday gazed up at the impressive buildings comprising the medical center where Tom worked.

"So, this is where you work."

"Yep. I do most of my work at St. Joseph's Hospital, which is part of the medical facility. Pediatric and adult cardiac surgeries take place St. Joseph's. We passed it a few minutes ago. I'll have to show it to you on the way back."

"Was it the old building, the one that looked like it was built in the early nineteenth-century?" she asked.

"That's the one," Tom said as he turned right on Broadway Street.

"You must love your job, since you spend so much time there."

Tom flashed a smile. "I do love my job. I've wanted to be a doctor since I played with my first stethoscope."

"And when was that?"

"Oh, I think I was about five. Dad gave me a toy

doctor kit. I was obsessed with it, always testing people's temps, listening to heart beats, and taking blood pressures."

Wednesday had an image of Tom as a little boy pretending to be a doctor. Big green eyes, curling black hair, and a toothless smile came to mind.

"I bet you were adorable."

"I drove my parents crazy. Whenever my mother coughed or sneezed, I'd pull out my doctor's bag and demand to take her temperature."

Wednesday laughed. "I can see you doing that."

"Dad was a doctor, so he understood my passion, but mom always hoped I'd choose a different profession."

"Why?"

"Because she didn't want me to follow my father's example."

"Did he work long hours, too?"

Tom nodded. His smile turned sad. "I barely saw him."

"Did he work at the same hospital?"

"Yeah. He was big into research, constantly at the lab trying to find cures for all diseases. I'm a third generation doctor. Grandpa worked there too."

"I haven't met your dad yet."

"He's away at a medical conference in San Diego this week. You'll meet him when he gets back. His first stop will be to see the kids. He spoils them rotten."

Wednesday couldn't resist placing a hand upon his arm. "Your kids may be spoiled, but they are not rotten," she told him softly. "Far from it."

"Thanks, I'll take that as a compliment."

"Please do."

"Here we are," he announced as they pulled through the front gates, paid a parking attendant, and looked for a space.

Swarms of people parked their cars and entered

the fairgrounds. "It's busy," Wednesday said, amazed at the comings and goings of groups varying from small to large.

"Packed. Maybe we should forget it," he said hopefully.

She laughed. "You're not getting out of it that easily."

"I know," he groaned.

"There's one," she cried out, pointing a finger to a spot just vacated by a minivan.

Tom pulled the car in and parked it. "I don't know if I'm ready for this or not."

Wednesday patted his shoulder. "Don't worry, I'll make sure you have a great time."

"I'm sure I'll enjoy time with you," he gazed at the midway where the bright lights of the carnival rides flashed, "but I'd rather not try out any of the rides."

They got out of the car. Wednesday circled around back and grabbed his hand.

"We are definitely going on rides." She gave his hand a tug. "You don't get sick do you?"

He shook his head. "I just prefer to keep my feet firmly planted on the ground."

"Do you fly?" she asked as they starting walking towards the entrance.

"Airplanes are different."

She giggled. His fright made him all that more loveable. A big, tall, strong doctor like him, afraid of dinky carnival rides. It was highly amusing.

"No difference at all," she said.

Screams echoed from the midway. His expression turned to one of absolute terror.

"There's a big difference," he grumbled. "Can't we go home? Or we could go to a movie."

"Come on. Loosen up."

"I don't even enjoy rides at Disneyland."

"I think we'll try the Tilt-A-Whirl first."

He grimaced. “I hate that ride.”

“But, you’ve never been on it with me. I’m fun.”

“I don’t see how being on it with you can change how I feel about that ride. It still spins you around until you feel sick to your stomach. And isn’t that the one where your neck gets yanked back against the seat as you turn round and round and round?”

“That’s the one,” Wednesday said ecstatically. She gave his hand another tug as they walked onto the crowded grounds. “Come on. I also want to ride the Scrambler and the Octopus and the Ferris Wheel.”

“Do we get to do any games?” he asked, as she pulled him toward a ride ticket booth. “I’m good at those,” he said.

Wednesday tossed a wide smile at him over her shoulder. “Only if you promise to win me a stuffed animal.”

“Deal.”

Tom told her he thought they bought way too many ride tickets, but Wednesday assured him he’d love the clunky carnival rides. He was adamant that he wouldn’t.

Wednesday didn’t share too many of the same interests with her family, but they all loved fairs and carnival rides. Her fondest memories were of time spent with her family on rickety roller coasters and eating fair foods. She always overindulged on the carnival food, and she couldn’t leave the grounds until she’d experienced her fair share of roasted almonds and cheese curds. Thankfully, she didn’t need to worry about her waistline.

The scent of greasy foods and thrill-frightened screams filled the air.

“Are you ready to try a ride?” she asked.

He halted. “Not yet.”

She grasped his hand. “I say you are.”

Tom moaned, dragging behind as Wednesday

pulled him toward the Octopus. "I'm having second thoughts about this."

Amazingly enough, there wasn't a long line. Wednesday handed the ride operator the correct number of tickets and stepped into the black contraption.

Tom stopped.

Wednesday shook her head at the wary look on his handsome face. "It's not the Tilt-A-Whirl."

He looked incredibly pale, and that was saying a lot, since he was quite tan.

"Can I sit this one out?" he asked.

"Don't be shy," she told him, giving the empty space beside her a pat. "I won't bite."

"You know it has nothing to do with you."

"This is one of the tamer rides," she assured him.

"Yes, but it still spins you around."

"They all do."

"Are you getting in, buddy, or not?" asked the operator gruffly.

Tom nearly jumped into the seat next to Wednesday.

The man grinned, revealing a mouth full of stained teeth. He slammed the door shut and double-checked to make sure they had safety belts locked.

Tom turned to Wednesday. "You enjoy this?"

She nodded and placed her hands on the bar in front of them. "Absolutely. There's something exciting about riding these rides."

"I don't see anything exciting about teasing death," he mumbled. He wrinkled his nose. "Besides, it doesn't smell too good in here."

It didn't smell that bad. She noticed he clasped the metal bar so tightly his knuckles turned white.

He stiffened as the car moved upwards.

"Haven't you ever been on the Octopus?" she asked.

"No." He sat up, ramrod straight. "To tell the truth, I haven't been on many fair rides. My parents weren't into it, and neither was Mary."

"Surely, you go to the Minnesota State Fair?"

He shook his head. "Never been."

"Well, we'll have to change that. It's one of the best state fairs in the country. I can't believe you've lived here your entire life and never been to the Great Minnesota Get Together."

He shrugged. "Never minded. I'm not one for crowds. I told you, I wasn't a fair type of guy."

"Well, I'm a fair type of girl, and you're stuck with me for the night."

"Looking forward to it." He winced as the car they were riding in made its first spin.

She gave his arm a playful slap. "You'll be just fine. It's perfectly safe."

"Yeah, right," he muttered.

Wednesday grinned. He looked petrified. She glanced over the side of the car, watching the people below get smaller as they climbed higher into the sky.

The ride picked up speed, until soon they flew through the air in a wide arc, their small black car whirling about in a tight circle.

Wednesday didn't want the ride to end. She liked the feel of Tom's body crushed against hers. With every spin she sank closer until her legs practically entwined with his.

But it did end, and when they came to a complete stop, he turned to her and asked, "Which ride is next?"

His question took her by surprise. "What did you just say?"

"Which ride is next?"

"I thought you hated rides."

"Well, I might be changing my mind. I never knew they could be so much fun." He looped his arm through hers and gave her a wink. "Of course, riding with you gives me a whole new perspective on carnival rides. You were right. You are fun."

It was obvious he'd enjoyed their closeness as much as she had. She grinned, hugging his arm to her side. "How about the Tilt-A-Whirl?"

"I guess. I still don't know about those flaming red cars twirling at a neck-break pace."

Wednesday grabbed his hand and pulled him forward. "Oh, it'll be fun."

"Will you still respect me if I lose the contents of my stomach all over your shoes?"

She glanced down at her open-toed shoes. The brilliant teal sandals were brand new, and she didn't care to get vomit on them. She could always magically return the shoes back to new if she wanted. Besides, Tom's enjoyment was more important than a pair of cheap shoes.

"I'll still respect you, Dr. Anderson," she said, "and I promise, I won't tell your daughters."

He wiggled his pointer finger at her. "You better not. I need to uphold my hero status in their eyes. Remember, I sign your paychecks."

Like money mattered to Wednesday. But Tom had no idea she could summon up cash at any time. It was frowned upon to do anything for personal gain, but everyone did it at one time or another. After all, what fun was magic, if you couldn't indulge yourself, now and then?

"Well, in that case, if you do upchuck on my feet, I think I deserve a raise," she teased.

He stared at her for a moment and then laughed. "Yes, I believe I owe you a raise even though you and my mother cuckolded me into coming to this poor excuse for a good time." He gestured at the scene around them. "Good thing I do have a strong stomach."

Wednesday dropped his hand, placing her hands

on her hips, she asked, "And what do you think is a good time?"

"A dinner in a nice restaurant, a good movie, and drinks afterwards," he answered. "Or a trip to the theater or opera or a museum."

"Those are nice, but not better than this."

"How so?"

"You can't compare them. An evening at the fair isn't in the same category as an evening at the opera."

"You can say that again," he snorted.

"I say they are too different to compare."

"I agree with that, about them being different."

Wednesday latched onto his arm again. "We're going on the Tilt-A-Whirl."

"Good thing I haven't eaten much."

"We're going on it twice, two times in a row."

"Ugh," he grumbled as he allowed her to pull him down the midway toward the bright blue and red ride.

She was having a blast, spending time alone with Tom.

Dusk fell as they ascended the rickety stairs to the Tilt-A-Whirl ride. The sun sank low on the horizon. Streaks of pinks and oranges and purples stretched across the summer sky. The heat of the late afternoon slowly gave way to the cooler temps of a summer night.

Wednesday plopped down on the torn vinyl seat, faded blue in color and patched with duct tape in a variety of places. She patted the empty space beside her. "Here have a seat."

"One of the highest quality," he commented, sarcasm in his voice, as he took his place beside her.

She rolled her eyes heavenward. "I'm beginning to think you're a snob."

"Just because I don't enjoy carnivals?" he asked, giving her a hurt look.

"We're going to slide an awful lot," she warned, "with only two people."

"But, that's the best part." He sat down next to her and snaked his arm around her middle.

The car began to pick up speed, and in no time at all, they twirled and whirled in tight circles.

Wednesday giggled uncontrollably as she slid down the seat and crunched into Tom. She had no control over it. She tried to reposition herself every time the swirling craziness subsided, but failed miserably. They'd chosen an excellent car. It didn't slow down for very long, turning around and around on its axis as the ride continued to spin in a circle.

"How do you like it so far?" she yelled at him after the finish of the most tantalizing spin yet.

"Horrid machine," he yelled back, but he looked like he was having fun.

Wednesday squealed as the car swept about the well-oiled track with the speed of lightning. She slammed into Tom again, but she didn't mind. She didn't mind at all. Being so close to him made her happy. She felt a little drunk on the euphoric excitement generated from the ride and from the close proximity to Tom's body.

Her legs quashed against his. The fabric of his pants rubbed against her bare leg. Her arm squeezed tightly against his from the gravitational pull of the ride as they twirled about. The hairs of his bare arm tickled her skin, and he covered her hand with his, holding on for dear life.

Wednesday grinned foolishly at him.

This is definitely my favorite ride.

The ride stopped sooner than either wished, but they hopped right back on for a second time around.

Ten minutes later, they stumbled down the exit steps, laughing so hard they clutched their aching stomachs.

"I don't think I can go on that ride again,"

gasped Tom. He leaned forward to try and catch his breath. "Please, don't make me go on it again."

"Okay, maybe not right now," Wednesday said, "but later."

Tom held up his hands and took a deep breath. "Not tonight. Not ever. I'm done on the Tilt-A-Whirl."

Wednesday's head pounded, and she still couldn't stand quite straight. She felt a tad dizzy and sick herself from the adventure on the Tilt-A-Whirl.

"No argument there," she conceded between gasps for breath, "but I wouldn't mind trying out the Scrambler."

"Now?" he asked incredulously.

"Okay, later," she agreed.

"Much later," his voice begged.

They grinned at each other.

"Agreed."

"So, what should we do next?" Tom asked.

"How about an introduction?"

Wednesday froze. There was no mistaking the voice. It was Tuesday. And Wednesday had no doubt her mother was somewhere nearby. This was too horrible for words. She'd wanted to avoid a family confrontation for as long as possible.

Members of her family were difficult to explain. Magic followed them everywhere.

Tom stared over Wednesday's shoulder. "Who are you?" he asked.

Wednesday took a deep breath and pasted on a smile before looking back over her shoulder.

It was Tuesday all right, dressed in a flowery blue skirt, t-shirt and sandals, her dark hair secured away from her face in bright-colored butterfly barrettes. Her companion was her incorrigible son Jasper, a blue-eyed, blonde-haired cherubic looking child who knew he was darn cute, and used it to his advantage.

"Hi, Weds."

"Hi, Aunt Weds!" shouted Jasper.

It was impossible to resist Jasper's impish smile. Wednesday grinned down at him. He was adorable. And he was sticky. Remnants of pink cotton candy hung at the corners of his lips. His little hands looked quite grimy, one grasped Tuesday's. He was five and loved everything and anything sweet, from chocolate to jelly beans.

"Hi." Wednesday glanced around nervously.

Tuesday laughed. "Don't worry. Mom is not here."

Wednesday breathed a sigh of relief. Okay, if a member of her family had to show up, she'd choose Tuesday. At least Tuesday was the most normal of the bunch, a result of being married to a mortal man. However, Jasper did not take after his mortal father. He was a warlock, with immature, newfound magic, random and uncontrollable at best. He could be a real mischief-maker.

Tom cleared his throat.

Wednesday blushed. "I'm sorry. I'm being rude."

Tuesday arched an eyebrow. "Yes, you are, rather."

Wednesday gave Tuesday a warning glare.

Tom stepped forward and stretched out a welcoming hand. "I'm Tom."

Tuesday took his hand, her smile warm. "I'm Tuesday, Wednesday's sister. Nice to meet you."

Tom turned his attention on the little boy. "And you are?"

"I'm Jasper." He jabbed a finger at Tuesday. "She's my mom."

Tom smiled. He offered his hand. "Hello."

Jasper took Tom's hand and gave it an overzealous shake. "Nice to meet you."

"And you," Tom chortled as he withdrew his

hand from Jasper's sticky clutches.

Wednesday bit her lower lip to keep from smiling at the slight look of horror on Tom's face when he saw the sugary goop left on his fingers.

"I was hoping to meet Wednesday's family at some point."

"Well, we're a little overwhelming."

"I think I can take it."

Tuesday grinned. "I suppose you can. So, you must be the doctor my sister is working for."

Tom's eyes met Wednesday's. "She's told you about me?"

"Oh, yes. She was very excited to get the position. You'll find she's wonderful with children."

Amusement sparkled in his eyes. "That she is. My girls love her."

"But she's rather awful at keeping in touch with her family. We haven't heard from her in weeks."

"I've been busy."

"Mmmm! Ice cream cone!" cried Jasper. He lunged away from Tuesday but she held his hand firmly. He looked back at her, brow furrowed, lower lip jutted out. "I want it."

"No."

"I can have it," Jasper declared.

Warning bells went off for Wednesday. Of course, he could have anything he wanted. All he had to do was think about it and the object of his desire would appear in his hand. His magic was out of control. It was a normal stage for young witches and warlocks, but it wouldn't be at all normal for Tom to witness.

Tuesday tugged him back to her side. "No. You've had enough treats tonight."

"Not fair." He looked up at Wednesday and turned on his I'm-so-cute-so-don't-deny-me smile. "Aunt Weds?"

Wednesday shook her head.

The smile vanished. Jasper sulked.

Wednesday swore she heard Tom chuckle. She didn't look his way, watching her nephew with trepidation.

It was difficult to raise a magical child in a mortal world. Wednesday didn't envy her sister that responsibility.

Tuesday rolled her eyes. "These places hold too much temptation. How many kids do you have again?" she asked Tom.

"Three girls."

"I have four, two boys and two girls. And they are quite the handful. I think it's time to call it a night."

Wednesday could tell by Jasper's expression and twitching fingers that he was about to do something that would be impossible to explain to Tom.

She met Tuesday's gaze. Unspoken understanding passed between them.

"Well, I should go," said Tuesday. "My husband has the other three and is probably losing his mind about now. Besides, we've been here long enough."

"It was nice to meet you."

"Nice to meet you as well, Tom. I hope we'll see each other soon." Tuesday stepped forward and wrapped one arm about Wednesday. "You'll pop in later and fill me in?" she whispered in Wednesday's ear.

Wednesday nodded, returning her sister's hug. Tuesday backed away, giving Wednesday room to kneel and hug Jasper who still wasn't one bit happy about not having ice cream.

"Bye, Jasper."

"Bye, Aunt Weds."

"Be a good boy."

He scowled.

Wednesday kissed his nose. "Promise me."

"Okay. I promise," he muttered reluctantly.

But Wednesday didn't believe him for one moment.

Tuesday pulled him away with gentle hands. "We'll see her soon, Jasper. Have a good night."

"Thanks. You too," said Tom.

Wednesday waved to Jasper until Tuesday and he disappeared around a corner. She felt she'd just evaded a major catastrophe.

"You have a nice sister."

"Yes."

"Not at all crazy," he teased.

She felt color flame her cheeks. "Not her, but there are others."

"Jasper seems quite the character."

She looked at Tom to determine his tone, but merriment shone in his eyes. She couldn't help but start to laugh.

"Oh, you have no idea," she giggled. "He's a headache, an adorable, rambunctious headache."

"I hope to get to know him better," said Tom, linking his arm with hers. "And the rest of your family."

Her heart warmed and she leaned into his side. "You don't know what you're asking."

"Oh, I think I do. So, what should we do next?"

There wasn't much to do except go on rides. They were directly in the middle of a very busy midway.

And, of course, there was fair food.

Her queasiness evaporated. She smelled bratwurst, hotdogs, and the sugary scent of cotton candy.

"I'm hungry."

He groaned. "The thought of food makes me want to hurl. I don't see how you can be hungry."

"Well, I am."

"Sounds like you have a lot in common with your nephew," he joked. "An insatiable appetite."

She pinched him.

"Ouch!" exclaimed Tom, drawing slightly away from her, although humor curved his lips into an a smile. "Can we wait just a little longer?" He rubbed his stomach. "My stomach's strong, but not as used to all this as yours is."

"As long as we don't wait too long."

"Can we wait an hour?" he asked hopefully.

"Thirty minutes?"

"All right, in thirty minutes."

"And then, we're going to pig out on fair food."

"Greasy, fattening, artery-clogging food?" He shook his head. "I don't think so. I'll eat something healthy."

Wednesday burst into laughter. "This is junk food heaven. You aren't going to find a salad or a cup of yogurt with granola crumbles."

"I've seen what this type of food does to the body." He shuddered. "It isn't pretty."

"Okay, I'll try to think of something healthy for you to eat," Wednesday chuckled as she added, "but, it'll be a challenge. So, what should we do for the next..." She glanced at her watch "...twenty-five minutes?"

"Play a game," he suggested, gesturing towards the row of games lining one side of the midway.

She eyed the array of stuffed animals with trepidation. They were always made of the brightest most horrid colors.

"So you can win me an ugly stuffed animal."

"Don't get your hopes up on the first try. It might take me a few times before I win anything."

"I thought you said you were an expert at the games."

"I said I was good," he corrected. "However, I'm out of practice and I'm not an expert. I haven't played midway games since high school."

Wednesday linked her arm through his. "I'm

interested in seeing how good you are. Which game would you like to play first?"

"I always had a knack for the shooting gallery."

"I'm surprised."

"Why?"

"You and guns. They just don't seem to go together."

"I hunted all the time when I was a kid. My grandpa had a cabin up north. We'd go on hunting and fishing trips together." Tom smiled at warm memories. "I miss him. He was a good man, and he always had time to be with me. I learned a lot from him."

"What type of doctor was he?"

"Obstetrician. That man loved babies and kids, and he was fantastic with women."

"How many babies did he deliver?" Wednesday asked curiously as they strolled along the lighted midway.

"Hundreds. He never retired. He practiced until he died. He always said he wouldn't know what to do with himself if he retired."

"How sad."

He looked down at her. "Why?"

"Because, he didn't get a chance to enjoy not working, having time for himself, enjoying hobbies and taking trips."

"Oh, he enjoyed life. He lived it to the fullest. Grandma and he took loads of trips. They took ballroom dancing, golfed and went fishing together. He was a great guy. I always wanted to be more like him. He found time to be with his family—to balance work and pleasure."

"He sounds like he was wonderful." He'd managed to find a balance in life, something Tom could take a lesson from. "Where's your grandma, now?"

"She moved to Arizona after he died. A bunch of

her widowed friends decided to move to Mesa. They're living it up in a retirement neighborhood. She's enjoying herself. Golfing every day, polka dancing every weekend."

"I'd like to meet her." Looked like he could learn a thing or two from his grandma as well. "She sounds incredible."

"I'm sure you will. She stays at the house when she visits. She'll be home for Christmas."

I won't be here at Christmas.

The thought saddened her.

"Can't wait," she told him with a forced smile. They stopped before a shooting gallery booth. "How about winning my animal, now?"

Tom paid the guy five bucks for three shots. He missed every single gunslinger. The shooting gallery had an Old West theme.

"I warned you, it had been awhile," he said sheepishly.

She returned his charming smile. "Try again."

He paid the booth attendant another five bucks and gave it a second try. No bulls' eyes.

"Third time's the charm," she encouraged.

"Or, three strikes and I'm out." He decided to try again.

On the third and final try, he managed to slay one gunslinger, hitting him square in the chest. The animated gunslinger flipped over, and Tom had his choice of medium-sized stuffed animals.

"Lady's choice," Tom said.

Wednesday pointed to a black cat with slanted green eyes. It resembled a Halloween cat with a high arching back and a tail standing straight up.

"I should've guessed you'd pick that one."

"He looks like Inky," Wednesday said, tucking the cat under her arm.

"The spitting image," Tom agreed.

"Inky is more loveable, though."

Tom arched an eyebrow. "That's a matter of opinion."

Wednesday reached up and gently pinched his nose. "Time to eat," she said.

They ordered a variety of fair treats.

"I feel my cholesterol rising twenty points just looking at the fatty food," he told her, grumpily, "and my arteries are protesting loudly."

She mostly ignored his comments. The one thing she didn't get was cotton candy, but only because the booth wasn't close by. She assured Tom, she'd be getting a large cotton candy by the end of the evening. For now, she settled for a bratwurst overflowing with ketchup, mustard and sauerkraut. In between bites of the spiced sausage, she popped a mini donut.

"Delicious," she gushed.

Wednesday saw amusement in his eyes. "What?"

"You have a bit of ketchup," he leaned forward and wiped it off her nose, "here."

"Not too ladylike, am I? I wouldn't fit in with your rich doctor friends. You're probably thinking you'd never take such a slob to the opera."

Tom smiled. "On the contrary, I'd gladly take you anywhere. I think you're a chameleon and change with your environment." He folded the napkin and put it aside. "Don't forget, I did see you in a very sexy and classy black dress at your five-course meal. Everyone adored you."

She was happy to hear he thought she'd looked sexy in the slinky black dress. "Except your fiancée."

"Anjelica is not my fiancée."

Wednesday shrugged as she took a long slurp of her large Coca-Cola.

That's what you think.

Men could be so blind sometimes, especially when it came to matters dealing with drop-dead gorgeous blondes. Wednesday liked to refer to it as the Marilyn Monroe Syndrome.

But she kept her mouth shut. She didn't want to ruin their perfect night with talk of Anjelica, and she cursed herself for bringing up the woman's name.

"I hope she's feeling better," he said.

Wednesday didn't. She saw Tom cast a distrustful glance at the corn dog on his plate. "You can eat it," she encouraged. "You aren't going to die or anything."

"Pizza is it for me in the junk food category."

Wednesday waved her hand in the direction of a pizza stand. "You can get that instead. I'll eat your corn dog."

"You sure have a large appetite."

She dabbed her lips with a napkin and reached for his corn dog. "I'm not quite sure if that's a compliment or not."

"Take it as one."

"I will. Thanks."

****

After Wednesday devoured the disgusting looking corn dog, they walked over to the pizza booth. While Tom sunk his teeth into a pepperoni pizza, Wednesday bought a candied apple. She pranced towards him with her treasure. Her beaming smile made him want to kiss her again.

Damn! He was in a somewhat serious relationship with Anjelica. When she'd started talking about marriage, he felt like he was being pushed. The last few weeks had been rather strained between them. He should have broken things off, instead of allowing Anjelica to believe they had a future. He knew now, they didn't.

Things had changed drastically when Wednesday showed up on his doorstep, all pretty and funny and congenial. The green flecks of her eyes practically disappeared in their amber depths.

Now, her smile was more fabulous than ever.

Those dimples were more endearing, and she smelled wonderful, a mixture of lavender and lilac that was unique to her.

He desired her. His craving for her nearly bordered on being uncontrollable. She provoked a heated reaction in him with just a single glance. It'd been awhile since he'd felt such desire for a woman, even Anjelica failed to ignite such need.

"How's your pizza?" she asked.

"Delicious. How's your apple?"

"Scrumptious." She took a bite. "It's sort of nutritious. Want some?"

He shook his head. "No, thank you. Not a fan of sweets."

She pushed the candied apple at him. "Come on. Try something new."

He couldn't resist her. He bit off a sugary morsel. The treat really wasn't too bad. "It's better than I thought," he said.

She beamed happily. "I knew I could convince you to enjoy fair food."

"Maybe, I'd like mini-donuts better."

Wednesday shoved her nearly empty bag under his nose. "Oh, you'll like these for sure."

He gingerly took one and placed it in his mouth. Not bad. He could see why these tiny donuts could be addicting.

"Well?"

"Quite good," he admitted.

"We'll get you a whole bag," Wednesday said, turning towards the mini-donut vender.

He stopped her, grabbing the edge of her shirt sleeve. "A couple will be just fine. Baby steps."

"All right" she relented, looking back at him "but you have to promise to buy your very own cotton candy."

He'd be feeling sugar on his teeth all week long. "I cross my heart."

"So, what should we do next?" She finished off her donuts, crumpled the bag, and tossed it into a garbage can nearby.

"Another ride?" he suggested.

"The Scrambler or the Ferris Wheel?"

Egad! He couldn't imagine riding another one of the jolting rides. "The Ferris Wheel sounds perfect."

He tossed the remainder of his food in the garbage and took Wednesday's hand. They ambled off together at a casual pace, walking underneath the fluorescent lights of the midway.

They were soon seated on the Ferris Wheel, snuggled in tightly up against each other. The ride looked about one hundred years old with peeling white paint and broken lights, but it had a nostalgic appeal. It served as a reminder of a simpler, peaceful time, before wild roller coasters and massive water rides. Before the more expensive theme parks, and before the introduction of television and the rise in popularity of video games, the small county fairs entertained hundreds of people with only 4-H displays and a few unexciting rides like the Ferris Wheel.

It was a comforting ride.

Tom leaned back against the burgundy-cushioned seat. "Now this is my type of ride," he declared as the Ferris Wheel started moving into the night sky.

"I hope they stop us at the top," Wednesday said. She leaned to look at the crowd beneath, causing the cart to swing slightly. "That is the best. It's so quiet up there, away from it all."

The ride stopped a few more times as the operator let more people on. Finally, it began a slow and steady movement up through the air and back down to the ground.

Wednesday closed her eyes. Tom watched the wind ruffle strands of hair away from her face. She laughed as they floated around and around in a graceful arch, leaning her head back and opening her eyes, sighing with delight.

"Look at all the stars dotting the sky. Isn't it beautiful?" she asked softly.

Tom wasn't looking at the sky. He only had eyes for Wednesday.

"Yes," he whispered.

Wednesday turned her head.

Her slow, enticing smile did him in. Tom couldn't keep from kissing her any longer. He'd thought about kissing her all night. And now, she was smiling that fantastic smile. The dimples appeared in her cheeks. Small crinkles creased the corners of her laughing eyes, now a deeper shade of appealing green.

He leaned toward her.

The Ferris Wheel stalled at the very top.

Tom closed his eyes.

And time seemed to stop for one glorious moment as he covered her lips with his.

Wednesday curled against him, kissing him back, turning his gentle kiss hungry. The kiss started as tender, turned passionate and fiery, and then, warm and loving. He never wanted it to stop. He cupped her face in his hands. His fingers brushed her cheeks. He deepened his kiss, his fingers tangled in her hair. His lips moved ardently across hers. He could feel her heart beating with wild anticipation against his own.

And in one priceless moment, Tom discovered what he felt for Wednesday was more than lust. He loved her. He loved her with everything in him. He loved Wednesday Green with all his heart.

How had it happened? He'd only known her for three months, the amount of time it takes a summer to fly by. Had he ever believed people could fall in love so fast? Maybe not lately, and yet he had to admit he had for the second time.

He remembered now how he'd fallen fast for Mary, too. He'd loved her at first sight, knowing almost immediately she was the woman he was going to wed, the woman he wanted to share his life with, the woman he wanted to be the mother of his children.

He'd had to convince her of his love, but eventually he'd won her over. Oh, how he'd cherished all their years together, loving her more with each passing day.

And now, there was Wednesday.

She'd changed him. She'd broken the wall he'd built so strong and firm around him. Somehow, she'd managed to make him take chances again, to enjoy the simple pleasures in life, to realize there was more than work, and how much his daughters needed him in their lives, and, how he needed them.

Tom needed this woman in his arms, the one responding to his kiss, and holding him tightly to her.

He hoped the Ferris Wheel would break down, stranding them high above the fairgoers. He wished Wednesday could stay in his arms forever, with their lips touching, and their bodies entwined, while the stars glimmered above.

Tom's heart dropped when the Ferris Wheel moved, and they began the final descent.

He pulled away from her slowly, gazing down into her upturned face, watching the emotion flickering in her eyes.

He loved her. The realization shocked him to the bone.

Love came in unexpected packages. Wednesday Green was one of those packages.

He felt as if he'd known her forever, felt as if they were somehow, destined. It almost seemed as if some magical force gravitated them to one another, but he didn't believe in magic. To him, there was only reality.

She was the one person capable of making him question reality. Magic seemed to thrive around Wednesday Green. Yes, there was a magical quality to her. He couldn't explain it. It was impossible, but he knew there was something otherworldly about her.

His children recognized this magic immediately.

Even if he hadn't recognized her right away, his soul had recognized its mate.

"Wednesday, I—"

Wednesday touched his lips with gentle fingertips and smiled. "Shush. No words," she murmured.

"But I—

"No. Please don't speak. I don't want to talk. I want to feel the moment, treasure it for always."

He wanted to tell her he loved her.

She pressed her fingers against his lips. "No words, Tom."

He nodded. Later. There was time to tell her how he felt about her, later.

Wednesday snuggled up under his chin. She laid her head against his chest. He held her close, resting his cheek against her dark hair, treasuring the feel of her in his arms, and wishing the night would never end.

Chapter Eleven

"I've decided to take off an entire week from work," Tom announced, the next day over breakfast.

Wednesday nearly choked on a spoonful of cereal. "What? You? I can hardly believe you'd take one day off, let alone an entire week."

"I've decided that I'm long overdue." He poured himself a steaming cup of coffee. "I have to go into work for a few hours today in order to arrange everything."

"Will the hospital give you the time off with this short notice?"

He leaned against the countertop and blew on the hot coffee. "I don't think I'll have a problem. My co-workers have been trying to get me to take a day off for the past year. They'll practically push me out the door."

"Why this sudden change?" she asked.

"Are you complaining?"

"Of course not."

"I'm taking your words to heart," he said softly. "I should spend more time with my girls."

This was too good to be true. Wednesday grinned. She was accomplishing her task. The girls would be overjoyed to have their father to themselves for an entire week, which meant soon her job would be over soon, and she'd have to leave the Anderson home.

The very idea of leaving them broke her heart. She loved the girls as if they were her own daughters, and no man, mortal or immortal, could hold a candle to how she felt for Tom.

"I'm glad," she whispered. "Wait until you tell the girls. They should be down any minute."

He glanced at his watch. "It'll have to wait, unless they wake up in the next fifteen minutes. I'm running late already. I've got a lot to do. Promise me you won't tell them. I want to do it."

"I promise," she vowed.

"Thanks." He sipped his cooled coffee for a few minutes and studied one of the many newspapers strewn out over the counter.

Sitting in the kitchen with Tom discussing the girls over coffee and breakfast was blissfully domestic. Wednesday loved it. She loved normal, everyday mortal stuff.

She finished the cereal, sipped the last of the orange juice in her glass, and walked to the sink, brushing against Tom as she did so.

Heat sparked between them.

Their eyes locked.

Tom's fingers encircled her wrist.

"Tom, I—"

"About last night—" he began, his voice husky and low.

She shook her head. "You don't need to say anything. It was heavenly. I had the best time."

He gazed into her eyes. "I want to talk to you about what happened between us."

"We shared a beautiful moment," she said and smiled, "a magical moment."

"But, I have so much more to say."

She lowered her eyes and looked away. "Tom, you don't need to explain. Things just happened."

Tom brushed her temple with his lips.

Wednesday released a heavy sigh.

"I said I have so much to tell you, Wednesday."

"You don't need to say anything. No strings attached."

"Wednesday, I—"

"Hiya, Daddy."

Wednesday jumped away from him, the milk in the empty cereal bowl sloshed, dangerously close to spilling out all over the kitchen floor.

Inky and Jazz rubbed against her ankles, looking at the bowl, hunger in their eyes.

"Hiya, baby," Tom said.

Jenna walked into the kitchen, covering a big yawn with one small hand. She hoisted herself up onto a chair and asked for a bowl of her favorite cereal.

It was some ultra sugary concoction. "Since when do we have such a cereal in this house?" he asked.

"Since two days ago, when I went grocery shopping with the girls," Wednesday responded.

"More sugar?" he chuckled.

Wednesday shook a dishcloth at him. "Don't start with me. A person should enjoy all life has to offer, including sugar, in moderation."

Tom smiled at her over the rim of his mug. "I agree."

"You agree?" she asked, stunned by his easy surrender.

"Going to the fair last night with you convinced me, life is short, and we should enjoy it."

"Exactly my point." She returned his smile.

"Well taken."

Wednesday opened a cabinet door, found the cereal box, and gave it to Jenna, who thanked her sweetly before pouring a generous portion.

"Chocolate milk, orange juice, grape juice?" Wednesday asked, opening the fridge and peering inside.

"Chocolate milk," Jenna replied. She showered the rainbow colored cereal circles with white milk.

"Chocolate milk for breakfast?"

Wednesday closed the fridge door with her hip

and laughed at Tom's amazed expression.

"Would you like a bowl of Lucky Charms and a glass of chocolate milk?"

"I've already had my breakfast."

"A cup of coffee? Now, that's healthy!"

He laughed and sat down next to Jenna. "Very well, I'll enjoy a bowl of sugar."

Jenna leaned over and gave him a quick kiss on the cheek. She generously handed him the box of cereal and pushed the container of chocolate milk in his direction.

Wednesday rinsed out her bowl and glass, placing both in the dishwasher. She wiped her hands on a towel and turned to watch father and daughter, but she didn't really see them.

She was too busy thinking about last night. Her lips still flamed where his had touched hers, and she still felt the gentle softness of his fingers on her cheeks, on her lips, and running through her hair. She never tired of kissing him and knew she never would.

He seemed so intent on discussing what happened between them. What could he possibly say that would make a difference? Unless he wanted to tell he loved her.

Did he? She didn't think so. No doubt he desired her. He'd openly admitted he enjoyed being with her.

He doesn't love me. He couldn't possibly.

But what if he did? What if Dr. Thomas Anderson had fallen in love with her in such a short time, just as she had with him? The very idea sent Wednesday's heart fluttering. Could he? Could he love her?

Even if he did, what kind of future would they have together—being from two different worlds? Would he still love her and want her if he discovered the truth about her? Most mortals couldn't wrap their logical minds around the fact that witches and magic existed. Her sister's husband was an exception to the rule, but even he needed some time for it to sink in.

Wednesday poured a cup of coffee, watching Tom and Jenna out of the corner of her eye. He was an excellent father. She never tired of watching his interaction with his daughters. When he took the time, he gave them his full attention.

Jenna giggled at something he said, tilting her head to the side. The sunshine flooding through the window bathed her young face. Her brilliant blue eyes shined, and her smile was wide and adorable. She gave her complete attention to her father, treasuring every moment with him.

Wednesday was surprised to realize how much Jenna resembled her mother. All three girls resembled Mary greatly in the face and they were all fair-haired and light-eyed, but Jenna's blonde curls were the same honey-gold and her eyes the exact deep blue. And her smile was the duplicate of Mary's.

Tears smarted Wednesday's eyes when she thought of how difficult it must be for Tom to look into Jenna's face. There could be no doubt that he saw a younger version of his beloved wife in his daughter. That must have been devastating for him in the days following Mary's untimely death, but it was a wonderful thing to behold as well. Mary wasn't dead. She'd never really die. Jenna carried her mother with her, Mary's little piece of immortality.

"Good morning," cried Michaela. She traipsed in, dragging her teddy bear behind her, Inky and Jazz clutched to the poor toy's legs.

"How'd you sleep, munchkin?" Tom asked. He kissed her cheek and ruffled her unruly curls.

"Good."

Wednesday helped her into a chair. "Cereal?"

Michaela nodded. She rubbed her eyes with small fists and asked if they were going to the zoo again.

"Not today. Did you have fun at the zoo?"

"Loads of fun," she giggled. "I like my monkey."

"Wednesday picked it out for you," Tom said. He shoveled a full spoon into his mouth. "I think I prefer this to grapefruit and toast."

Wednesday laughed. "Where's Tamra."

"Sleeping. She likes sleeping," Michaela said through a mouthful of sugary cereal.

"Tamra is not a morning person, same as her mom."

"I've never been a morning person, either," Wednesday admitted. She took a seat at the table with Tom and the girls, cradling the cup of coffee in the palms of her hands.

Tamra appeared in the doorway.

"Good morning, sleepy head."

Tamra smiled at her dad. "Hi, Daddy."

Tom mussed her already tousled hair. "Now that I have you all together, I have something to tell you before I head off to work."

"Don't you have Sunday off?" Jenna asked.

"That's exactly what I want to talk to you about." Tom pushed his bowl of half-eaten cereal away and reclined in his chair. "I've decided to take the week off."

The girls' eyes grew as wide with surprise.

Wednesday was startled again by how much all three resembled Mary. Jenna was a dead ringer, but the other two also looked like their deceased mother.

"What do you think about that?"

"An entire week?" Jenna asked incredulously.

"An entire week."

"Yippy!" Tamra cried. She clapped her hands and bounced up and down in the chair.

"I guess you won't be needing me this week."

Tom turned his eyes on her. "You aren't going anywhere. I want to spend time with all of you."

Wednesday's heart lurched. "Really?" she whispered.

"We are a family," Jenna piped.

"Yes, a family," Tamra repeated.

Tom's tender smile caused Wednesday's heart to pick up speed.

"You are part of this family. Don't ever forget it. I owe you more than I can ever repay."

"I didn't do anything," she murmured.

His eyes caught and held hers. "You've done more than you know. I say you've gone above and beyond the call of duty."

"I just want to see you and the girls happy."

"And we will be. We are happy, aren't we girls?"

"Yes!" Jenna, Tamra and Michaela chorused.

Wednesday's heart overflowed with love.

"So, what should we do?" Tom asked the girls.

"First, we have to have another tea party."

Wednesday grimaced. "I don't think so, Jenna."

"Why not, because I broke a promise?"

"You should never break a promise," Tom scolded gently.

Jenna hung her head. "I'm sorry, Wednesday. I didn't mean to."

Wednesday gave her a loving hug. "I forgive you, darling, but no tea parties with Alice and the gang for a long time."

"Okay," sighed Jenna, "but I had a really, really, really good time."

"Me, too." Wednesday planted an affectionate kiss on the cheek.

"Would I enjoy these tea parties?" Tom asked.

Wednesday shook her head. "Nope. I think you'd be overly bored."

"What else do you want to do?"

The girls started to chatter instantaneously

about all the activities they wanted to do.

Wednesday sipped coffee and smiled, listening to their array of ideas. By the time Tom left for the hospital, the entire week was planned out. His week off was jammed full with outings.

And the week ended up being very busy. They went school shopping, visited the park daily, swam in every pool in town, and journeyed to the Twin Cities to tour the Minnesota Science Museum. They also watched a variety of movies, played games, and went for long bike rides through the shady streets of the city.

It was all fun stuff. And by the end of the week, Wednesday knew she'd succeeded in her job. The girls were happy, Tom was happy, and they were spending loads of time together.

Occasionally, Wednesday worried Lumina would appear and whisk her away to some other job. Luckily the little fairy stayed away, and Wednesday was allowed to enjoy precious time with Tom and his daughters. She knew her hours were numbered. She was fulfilling her goals. Tom was spending more time with the girls and the family unit seemed reconnected, every member smiling and laughing and joyful.

The week flew by, and before Wednesday realized it, only one day of Tom's last minute vacation remained.

"I forgot how much fun it is to take time off," said Tom.

"You'll have plenty more."

"Yeah, but I shouldn't take it all at once."

"Tom, they'd understand."

Tom threw a bag of popcorn into the microwave. They'd just finished tucking the kids into bed. "It's nice to finally spend time alone with you."

She leaned against the counter. "I agree."

Being alone had never worked out. His mother

stopped by more times than necessary. His father surprised them with a visit after getting back into town from his conference, and a few of his co-workers invited themselves over, wanting to meet the famous nanny he raved so much about.

Tonight was the first night all week that they'd be alone together.

"Work was the only thing keeping me going after Mary died, keeping me sane." He punched in the minutes on the microwave's keyboard.

"What about the girls? Didn't they help you through?"

"Yes, but without my work I would've disappeared into this horrible place. I can't explain it to you. You have to experience it to understand that black, horrid, and desolate place. I hope you never do."

Wednesday had never experienced losing a family member, a loved one. She seldom thought about sickness, disease, or death because it never directly affected her. She couldn't imagine losing her brother or sisters, her mother, or any other member of her illustrious family. Even witches had a lifespan. Thankful they lived hundreds of years longer than the average mortal, and even though they drove her bonkers the majority of the time, she couldn't imagine a world without them.

"I can't recall ever losing someone close to me."

"No one. Not ever?"

She shook her head, sweeping a pile of crumbs off the countertop with a wet dishcloth.

"Everyone has lost someone."

"Not me, at least not that I remember." She shook the cloth over the sink, a few crumbs falling against the stainless steel basin.

"Are your grandparents still alive?"

"And doing very well," she said.

"How old are they?"

Wednesday stalled before giving her answer. How could she tell him their true age? Both were over two hundred years old. She couldn't possibly explain that.

"Let's just say, people in my family live a long time."

"It must be good genes, because it can't be your eating habits."

Wednesday loved how his eyes twinkled when he teased her.

"I do have good genes. I'm positive I'll live past the age of ninety."

"That's quite impressive. Most of my relatives keel over by the time they're eighty."

Wednesday rinsed off the cloth and draped it over the faucet. "You really shouldn't say such things."

"Why? I'm telling the truth."

"You might jinx it for yourself."

"Nah, I'm already jinxed."

The short life of mortals hit her hard. She wobbled on her feet and sat down in a chair. Her hands trembled. She slid them between her knees. She was clammy, cold and sick. Losing Tom to the Grim Reaper never occurred to her before. She always knew she'd live longer, but before now, she never thought about him actual dying. He'd grow old and feeble, and he would die. He was mortal. There was nothing she could do to fend off the wings of death. Witches couldn't interfere in the life and death cycle. It was beyond their magic. She shivered uncontrollably.

"Wednesday, are you okay?"

Wednesday gazed up into his concerned emerald eyes, and the pain in her heart grew tenfold.

"I'm fine."

"You don't look fine." He knelt in front of her, taking her clenched hands in his own. "Tell me what's wrong."

She looked away. Her entire body trembled. "I'm fine. Really, I am."

Tom held his hand to her forehead. "Maybe I should take your temperature."

She laughed a hollow little laugh. "I'm fine. Honestly, you don't have to worry."

"I do worry about you. Are you cold? Do you want a blanket?"

She nodded.

"We'll get you all snuggled up cozy on the couch in the family room in no time."

He lifted her off the floor and into his strong arms. She didn't fight him. She didn't want to fight him. She wanted to be close to him, to hear his healthy heartbeat, to be reassured he wasn't going to die on her any time soon.

Tom couldn't figure out why Wednesday was freezing. It was over eighty degrees outside with high humidity and the air conditioning was going at full blast. He hoped she wasn't getting sick.

"Maybe you've caught Anjelica's bug."

She shook her head. "No. I don't think so."

Tom set her on the sofa. He draped a cuddly fleece blanket over her shivering body.

A shrill beep vibrated through the house.

"The popcorn is done."

"It can wait," he said, sitting down beside her on the couch.

He tucked the blanket about her body. Slow warmth began to spread from the tips of her toes and up her legs.

"I'm feeling much better," she assured him. Her belly rumbled. "I could use some food."

"You are a bottomless pit."

She rubbed her belly and grinned. "I really do feel dandy."

"But something happened."

"I guess it was all the talk about death. I don't do well with that subject."

"Neither do I. How about we agree to not talk about it again." He offered his hand. "Deal?"

Wednesday shook his hand. "Agreed. Now go get that popcorn."

Tom abandoned her for the kitchen.

Thankful for a moment alone, she took a few deep breaths and tried to calm her frayed nerves. Her heart slammed hard against her ribcage.

He wasn't away for very long. "Here we are. I have popcorn with extra butter and a glass of water."

"You're very sweet." She took the water and grabbed a handful of popcorn.

"Are you positive you feel better, now?"

"Oh, yes, very." She munched on a few kernels.

"Do these episodes happen to you often?"

"I've never had one before."

"Can you explain to me how you felt?"

She told him.

"That sounds similar to a panic attack," he observed. A frown creased his brow. "I still think you might want to go in and get checked out."

"Death bothers me," she said softly. "I thought we were done talking about it."

"I could get you in tomorrow. I can pull strings."

She held up a hand to ward him off. "I don't do doctors."

It took a moment, but the serious look of concern in his eyes disappeared, replaced by the twinkle Wednesday loved so much.

"You don't *do* doctors?" he asked, a teasing lilt in his voice.

She knew what he implied. She gave his arm a playful punch. "You know what I mean, you dirty doctor."

A lopsided grin tilted his lips. "I hope you

change your mind."

"About doing doctors?"

"Yes."

"I doubt it."

"Not even for me?"

She shook her head and took a sip of water. "Not even for you, Dr. Anderson."

"I think I can change your mind."

Wednesday sank further into the sofa cushions. "You think so?"

"I know so." Tom removed the glass of water from Wednesday's hand and set it on the coffee table. "Ah, Wednesday, I've waited this entire week to be alone with you."

"You have?" she squeaked.

She'd tried hard to keep her distance from him after the night on the Ferris Wheel. It was just too hard to be near him.

"There's so much I have to say to you."

His voice dropped to a tantalizing low rumble, husky and mesmerizing. Her body gravitated toward his. The popcorn bowl tipped over in her lap, golden popped kernels scattered in every direction.

"We've been in this place before," she whispered. "On this couch, with popcorn, kissing."

"But that was when you were just the nanny."

His breath tickled her ear.

"What am I now?"

"The woman I love."

Wednesday couldn't believe her ears. "What? Wh—what did you say?" she sputtered.

"I love you."

He kissed her. It was the sweetest of kisses, his lips soft and light against hers. His fingers gently splayed across her neck.

She pulled away, gazing up at him with her eyes wide. "You love me?"

He nodded.

That slow, easy, wonderful smile turned up the corners of his mouth. Wednesday's heart did somersaults.

"But, what about Anje—"

Tom silenced her with a finger pressed against her lips. "All over. I broke it off with her at the beginning of the week."

"You did?" she asked, astounded.

"I did."

"I can't believe this."

"Believe it."

He kissed her again.

Wednesday's bare toes curled under the fleece blanket. She dragged her fingers through his black hair and kissed him back.

"I have to know," he whispered against her ear.

"Know what?" she murmured, her voice thick with emotion.

"Do you love me?"

What a foolish question! She burst into laughter and kissed him again and again, showering his handsome face with hundreds of kisses.

"Of course, I love you. I think I fell in love with you that very first day when you told me I wasn't qualified for the job."

"Hey, you seemed a bit suspicious to me."

Wednesday hugged him tight. There were so many reasons to push him away, but she couldn't. She loved him. And he loved her. Nothing else seemed to matter at that moment.

"I love you! I love you! I love you!" she shouted happily.

"I love you back."

He pushed her deeper into the sofa, his body sprawling across hers, kissing her so passionately tears burned her eyes. She moved beneath him, wanting him. Tonight, they'd consummate their love. She was ready, determined to show him how much she wanted him as hot desire flamed in her belly…

"Daddy? Wednesday? I don't feel too good," the sad little voice stopped them.

Wednesday bolted upright. Tom did the same. Both turned to the doorway where a sleepy-eyed Michaela rubbed her eyes. She was so tired that she hadn't even noticed their intimate embrace.

They jumped off the couch at the same time and ran to her side.

"Is it your tummy, darling?" Wednesday asked, taking Michaela in her arms.

Michaela nodded. "It hurts."

"Do you want to sit on the couch with us and watch a movie."

"Yes."

Tom and Wednesday exchanged smiles over the top of her curly head.

"We'll watch a movie with you, munchkin."

Wednesday carried Michaela to the couch. They snuggled up together under the blanket. Tom cleaned up the popcorn, got Michaela a glass of soda to calm her stomach, and popped in the requested movie. He settled next to them and draped his arm behind Wednesday. She leaned back against him, her body still throbbing from their encounter on the couch.

"Later," Tom promised with a whisper.

She blushed from the heated suggestion lighting his eyes.

"Later." She nodded and cuddled up against him. She couldn't wait until later.

Chapter Twelve

Later never came.

Michaela refused to go to sleep in her own bed, insisting she sleep in her father's.

Tom reluctantly agreed, gathering her up in his arms and carrying her to his bedroom, while making sure Wednesday knew falling asleep next to a sick three-year-old, no matter how adorable, was not what he'd had in mind. He loved his daughter dearly, but tonight he preferred his earlier plans of going to bed with Wednesday and not getting a wink of sleep.

Wednesday followed them up the stairs, carrying Michaela's ratty bear and a glass of ice water. She was disappointed not to be spending the night with Tom, but there'd be other nights. Perhaps they'd get a chance to be alone tomorrow.

"I'm real sorry about this," Tom said.

Wednesday lounged against his dresser while he pulled back the covers on his king-sized bed. She liked his room. It was decorated in dark greens and blues. Colorful area rugs covered the hardwood floor. It was a huge room with large picture windows overlooking the gardens and backyard, a comfortable sitting area with two oversized leather chairs, and a gigantic master bathroom, which was larger than her bedroom in the guest cottage.

"She can't help it. Poor thing."

Michaela curled up onto her side under the sheets. She wiggled her fingers at Wednesday. "Night, night."

"Goodnight, sweetheart. Sweet dreams."

Wednesday leaned over and placed a motherly kiss on Michaela's forehead. "Here's your teddy."

Michaela wrapped her arms around the toy and gave it a crushing hug.

"Close your eyes and try to go to sleep."

Tom took the glass of water from Wednesday and set it on the small table beside the bed.

"You don't have to go. We could talk."

Wednesday smoothed wild curls away from Michaela's cheeks. She tucked them behind the little girl's pixie-like ears.

"I think it'd be best if I left. I'll spend the night in the guesthouse."

"I'd rather have you here with me."

He lifted her hair off her neck and trailed sizzling kisses up and down her skin.

"Tom, we'll have time tomorrow night."

"Unless Mom stops by or Dad or some uninvited co-workers," he grumbled.

"Frustrated?"

"You know I am."

Wednesday turned into his arms. She laid her head against his chest and listened to the steady rhythm of his heart.

The house was silent around them.

"Tom, I want you to know I've had a really good time this week."

"Me too. I can't remember when I had so much fun."

Wednesday tilted back her head. She traced a faded scar on his cheek with her fingertips. The coarse bristles of his five-o-clock shadow tickled the sensitive tips.

"I need to shave."

"I kind of like it." She stood on tiptoe and pressed her lips against his. "I'm going to go."

"At least I know you're not far."

"Just a hop, skip and a jump away." She kissed

him again before stepping out of the circle of his arms. "I'll see you in the morning."

"I'm curious."

"Curious about what?"

"If we'll get to spend time together, alone time, tomorrow."

"How about, we make a date?"

He grinned. "Nine o'clock on the couch in the family room. I'll bring the popcorn."

"I'll choose the movie."

"We've got a date."

Wednesday laughed softly. "I'm looking forward to it."

She turned to leave.

He grabbed her hand.

She spun around and looked into his dark green eyes.

"Tom—"

He kissed the inside of her wrist and slowly, enticingly rained a hot path of delicious kisses up and down her arm.

Wednesday glanced at Michaela, but the three-year-old was fast asleep. She whispered, "I love you."

His eyes blazed a fiery green. "I love you, too."

Her breath caught in her throat. They definitely had chemistry. The bedroom would not be a problem in their relationship.

She gave him a quick peck on the cheek even though she wanted to throw him down on the bed and make love to him. "Goodnight."

He gave one more tantalizing kiss in the crook of her arm before she managed to free herself from his grasp. "I'll look forward to seeing you tomorrow."

"You'll be in my dreams," she whispered.

"And you'll be in mine." His voice dropped an octave, low and sensual.

Wednesday stepped out into the hallway, closing the door behind her, and took a deep breath. It took a great deal of willpower for her to move away from Tom's bedroom door. She could hear him moving beyond the closed door. He was most likely getting undressed. A vivid picture of him naked flashed in her mind. She hurried down the hallway, down the stairs, out the back door, across the lawn, and into her temporary house—away from temptation.

The feeling of his erotic kisses still lingered, branding her arm as she dressed for bed. She slid her silk nightgown over her head and sat down in front of the small vanity. As she dragged a brush through her long hair, she smiled, thinking of his lips against her neck.

Dr. Tom Anderson loved her. It was too fantastic to be true, but it was. She'd never felt so happy in all her life, and she had lived a very long time.

Wednesday stared dreamily into the mirror, lazily thinking what it would be like to be Mrs. Tom Anderson. "Wednesday Anderson," she murmured to her reflection.

Her family would be horrified to find out how much she enjoyed the thought of marrying a mere mortal and taking his name. They'd be more than disgruntled when another of their daughters announced being in love with a mortal man.

Her family had been hard on Tuesday when she married an earthbound man. They'd be nearly impossible to deal with if Wednesday decided to do the same thing. Right now, she didn't want to think of the consequences of loving Tom. She only wanted to enjoy the ecstasy coursing through her veins.

She discarded the brush and hopped into bed. Too excited to fall asleep, she materialized a book from thin air-fluffed the pillows behind her, and burrowed down for a good read.

Despite the intriguing story, she started thinking about Tom again. Barely having finished one page, she imagined him holding her. She'd much rather dream about Tom than read some boring old book. She turned off the light and curled up under the cool sheets, hugging a pillow against her body. She closed her eyes and willed sleep to come, hoping to meet Tom in her dreams.

****

A shrill voice shouting, "Good morning!" woke Wednesday abruptly the next morning, causing her to fall out of bed in startled surprise. She groaned as she hit the hard floor with a soft thud.

"Lumina, what are you doing?"

The little fairy danced around in the air. She spun, dipped, and pirouetted. Her wings fluttered gold and blue, pink and violet in the sunlight.

"I've got news for you."

"Good news I hope."

Lumina nodded her miniature head and flew up close to Wednesday's face.

"Congratulations."

"On what?"

"You've completed your first job with great success. The head honchos at the Foundation can't stop raving about you." Lumina grinned proudly. "Of course I did give them positive reports about you."

Wednesday sat up on the floor, pushing her hair away from her eyes. "What does that mean exactly?" She wasn't ready to leave the Anderson household. She never wanted to leave Tom and the children.

"Aren't you thrilled?"

"Lumina, what happens next?"

"Off to another job!" Lumina threw a piece of parchment at Wednesday.

Wednesday grabbed the tiny piece of paper. She squinted at it, barely able to read the words printed on it. "I can't read it."

Lumina twirled her wand and pointed it at the document. A burst of fairy dust fell on the parchment, and it grew four times its size.

Wednesday quickly read it over. The Magical Nannies for Children Foundation declared her a capable nanny and the board members were most impressed with her quick progress with the Anderson children and their father.

She couldn't help but feel pride as she read over the kudos for a job well done. The compliments were better than she ever imagined. It was more than she had dared to hope for...and worse.

Her heart filled with dread when she read the bottom few lines.

The Foundation had reassigned her to another family. They instructed her to pack her bags, say her goodbyes to her current charges, and leave as soon as possible—by no later than this evening.

"This family has major problems," Lumina said, tapping the instructions. She sat on the bedside table and swung her little legs over the edge. "The mom and dad are divorced, and the kids are selfish and rotten. They never listen and they've been spoiled. Dad's a big movie producer and Mom's a supermodel."

"Sounds like fun," Wednesday muttered sarcastically.

Lumina tilted her head. "What's the matter? I thought you'd be happy."

Wednesday glanced up from the official document. She let it drop to the floor. Tears filled her eyes and blurred her vision.

"I don't want to go."

Lumina hugged her legs to her chest. "It's that man."

"Yes."

"You shouldn't have involved yourself with him."

"How can I deny the feelings I have for him?" Wednesday asked. "I'd be betraying myself if I did that. There is something between us, something beautiful and precious and amazing. I can't turn my back on it."

Lumina clucked her tongue. "This is not good. This is not good at all. I've tried my best to keep this a secret, but if the Board finds out about this, they'll kick you out of the Foundation forever."

"You encouraged me."

"I most certainly did not!" Lumina exclaimed indignantly.

"Yes, you did. Don't deny it."

Lumina blushed and hung her head. "Okay, I did help. I even got rid of that annoying Anjelica."

Wednesday's eyes widened. "You did?"

Lumina nodded. ""She wasn't good for him and she was mean to you."

"What did you do to her?"

"Oh, I employed a warlock to sweep her off her feet. It won't last, of course, but it provided a nice distraction for a while, giving you and the doctor some time together without her constant interference. And then he broke it off. I don't think she was too upset. She has her hands full."

Wednesday clapped a hand over her mouth to stop the cascade of giggles. "Oh, Lumina! Thank you."

"I had to get involved." The fairy grinned. "I care about you and I've always had a soft spot for lost causes."

Wednesday lowered her hand. "Am I a lost cause?"

"No, but your relationship with the doctor is. You don't have a future with him."

"I could."

Lumina's eyes widened. "Are you willing to give everything up for him? Everything you've worked for?"

"Yes."

"Okay, so you'd quit your position as a nanny to be with him and his children, but that doesn't change the fact you are a witch and he is a mortal." Lumina fluttered off the table. "What do you think he'll say when he discovers your secret?"

"I don't know."

"Many mortals can't accept magic of any kind. They're frightened of it because they can't do it and don't understand it. So, they choose to believe it doesn't exist."

Wednesday thought about Tom and the girls—their laughter and smiles—their warmth.

"That's because they don't need magic, Lumina, at least not the kind of magic you and I conjure up."

"What other type of magic is there?"

Wednesday rose to her feet and walked to the window. She had a clear view of the main house from the bedroom. She leaned her elbows against the windowpane ledge.

"I can't explain it. A special magic exists for humans. It lives in their normal day-to-day lives."

"But they can't perform spells."

"No. But maybe what they have is more wondrous. After all, remember we can't mess with life and death or with love. These three things are more powerful than any spell I can cast."

"I suppose so."

Wednesday laughed at Lumina's doubtful expression.

"You have to leave. If you want to continue your job as a magical nanny, you have to have move on."

"Did I tell you he loves me?"

Lumina shook her head.

"He does."

"Well, that complicates things immensely."

"And…I love him."

"That makes it even more complex."

Wednesday sighed and turned away from the window. She'd known this day would come.

"I'll pack, Lumina."

"Good."

"But I'm going to tell him. I'm going to tell him everything."

"Do you think that's wise?"

"I do."

Lumina fluttered up to the window. "He might not believe you. He might decide you've lost your mind and throw you out of the house."

"What difference would it make? He might," Wednesday agreed. "But I hope not."

"He could be terrified of you once he learns you have powers."

"Yes, he may be. But I doubt it."

"What will you do if he believes you and loves you anyway?"

The corners of Wednesday's mouth tilted up into smile. "Unpack and love him for the rest of my life."

Lumina patted Wednesday's shoulder. "I wish the best for you. I hope it works out. I truly do."

"It worked for my sister," Wednesday reminded the fairy.

"As I said before, she was an exception. Many witches have fallen in love with mortals over the centuries, but those relationships seldom worked after their secret was discovered." Lumina bounced off the windowsill, hovering a few inches from Wednesday's nose. "Remember the witch hunts in England? Europe? Salem?"

"People with paranoia."

"Yes, but did you know each obsessive hunt started with the romance between a mortal and a witch?"

Wednesday's eyes widened. "No one ever told me that."

"Only a few mortals can accept such a secret."

"And I think Tom is one of them."

"I hope so for your sake."

"He'll accept me for who I am."

Lumina lightly kissed the tip of Wednesday's nose. "I wish you luck. I truly do. I don't want your heart to be broken."

"Thanks, Lumina."

"Your mother is going to freak out when she finds out about this."

"Don't you dare tell her. She needs to hear it from me."

Lumina grinned. "I won't say anything. I don't want to be the bearer...See you soon."

Wednesday waved goodbye, watching the little fairy vanish into the blue summer sky.

Nerves churned her stomach. She wanted to have faith in Tom. Deep down inside her heart she knew he wouldn't turn his back on her once he found out about her secret. But a slight niggling doubt had her worrying. What if he did? What if he didn't love her enough to accept her as a witch?

"I won't think about that," she whispered. "I can't think about that. He'll love me enough. I know he will."

Nevertheless, she was frightened. She didn't know what Tom's reaction would be. There was no guarantee.

Wednesday flung herself across the bed and pulled the covers up over her head. She wanted to stay in bed for the entire day, ignore the Foundation's instructions, and avoid Tom. But she knew she couldn't. She had to face him. She had to tell him the truth and deal with the consequences.

One hour later, she forced herself from the warm cocoon of her bed, dressed, and headed up the winding path to the main house where Tom awaited. She wasn't sure how she was going to approach the topic. How should she break the news to him? She couldn't think of the right words to say.

How did she tell the love of her life she was a cauldron-boiling, spell-casting, potion-making witch?

It was a pretty big secret. How would he react to the knowledge he'd trusted a witch with his children?

She wasn't the Wicked Witch of the West, but mortals had preconceived ideas about how witches should look and act, thanks in large part to the stereotypical Halloween witch—wart-ridden skin, long nose, ugly features, pointy hat, cackling laughter, and nasty hexes.

"We get a bad rap," she mumbled, opening the back door and stepping into the house. "That needs to be changed."

Tom was cooking in the kitchen, standing over the stove with a variety of utensils and pans cluttered about him. She paused in the hallway, hidden in the shadows. He was a breakfast she could devour. He was dressed in striped pajama bottoms and a faded blue T-shirt, his feet bare and his hair disheveled from sleep.

I could watch him all day.

He was altogether yummy. And he looked content, relaxed, and so very happy. She hated to ruin the moment.

A classic Beach Boys' song blared from the radio. She smothered a laugh when he started singing the lyrics and doing a few dance steps. He was rather good, but she found it extremely funny to catch him dancing and singing in his pajamas.

She stepped out of the shadows.

Tom spun around. The lyrics to the song died on his lips. He grinned crookedly, waving a spatula at her. "You shouldn't sneak up on people."

"I didn't want to interrupt," she laughed.

"You didn't know I liked to sing and dance in my jam-jams?"

"Jam-jams?"

"That's what Michaela calls pajamas."

"You look very handsome in your jam-jams, Dr. Anderson." She flirted with him. She couldn't stop. It was far too much fun.

"I'm looking forward to seeing your jam-jams."

Wednesday felt her entire face glow red. She took a step closer to him. "What are you making?"

"I'm trying to make Mom's famous blueberry pancakes."

Wednesday raised an eyebrow at the chaotic disorder across his countertops. "How's it going?"

He made a face. "Not so good. I guess I don't have the knack Mom does." He twirled his spatula. "Do you dare try some?"

Wednesday pulled out a chair and sat down. "I'd love to be your guinea pig."

He eagerly obliged her, piling a plate full of fluffy cakes.

Wednesday took a bite, chewed, and swallowed.

"Well?"

"Actually, quite good. Your mother would be proud."

Tom picked up a fork, reached across the table, and speared a generous portion. He smiled at the first taste. "Not bad. Not bad at all."

"Have the girls tried them yet?"

"My first batch wasn't quite so tasty. They took one look and ran screaming for the family room. Literally."

Wednesday covered her smile with the back of her hand. "I missed out."

"Decided to sleep in?"

"Yeah. I couldn't get my body out of bed this morning."

"Don't worry. I can take care of the girls by myself. Maybe you'd like a few hours off today."

"Not necessary."

"But you don't get the night off. We have big plans. Remember?" His exaggerated, flirtatious wink made her smile.

Boy, did she ever. "A night on the couch with

popcorn and a movie."

"...and *other* things." The promise in his husky tone of voice sent excited tingles racing up and down her spine.

But there wouldn't be a date tonight. She had to leave A.S.A.P. The Magical Nannies for Children Foundation wanted her gone by the end of the night.

"Tom, about that."

"You aren't going to back out on me now. We have unfinished business."

Wednesday lowered her head. She dropped her fork. It clattered on the table and fell to the floor.

"I'm not going to be here tonight." Her voice cracked.

"What's wrong?" His tender concern caused tears to fill her eyes. "Wednesday, please talk to me." He dragged a chair next to her and sat beside her. "What's happened?"

"I have to leave tonight." She clasped her hands tight in her lap. "My job is over."

Tom stared at her in astonishment. "What do you mean, you have to leave? What are you talking about? You're not leaving."

"I must." She raised her head and looked into his eyes.

"You can't leave me. You can't leave the girls." He grabbed her hands. "We love you."

"I have to go. I've done what I came to do."

"What was that?"

"Happiness. Joy. Love. Things you forgot about."

Happiness. Joy. Love. Mortal magic.

He smiled lovingly. "I won't argue. You helped heal us, but it'd break the girls' hearts if you left us now and mine." He touched his forehead and nose to hers. "Don't get scared away, Wednesday Green, even if my pancakes are atrocious."

"They aren't that bad. I'd tell you if they were."

"I'm scared too. I'm terrified." He kissed the

indentation below her nose. "I can't believe how blessed I am. I thought I'd never love again after I lost Mary. And then you walked into my life. And I'm afraid, so very afraid of losing you."

Wednesday caressed his cheek. "You don't need me anymore."

"Of course I need you. Don't you know how important you are?" He kissed the corner of her mouth. "I know what's wrong. You're frightened, scared to love. Want to know a secret? So am I. I lost one love. I didn't want to go through the pain of losing someone I love again, but you make me want to love again. I love the prospect of being in love and I'm excited to be in love again, to be in love with you. You are an amazing, wonderful, fabulous woman."

"Thank you." Wednesday took a deep breath. "Except, there is something you don't know about me."

"Just one thing?" His mouth curled up at the corners. "That's not bad."

"Don't joke. I'm serious." She pushed at his chest with the palms of her hands. "This is something huge, and it might change your mind about me, about us."

"Promise me you aren't going to leave."

"I can't promise you that. And you may think differently once I tell you."

"Impossible. Trust me. I'm not going to stop loving you, Wednesday. I want you in my life forever."

Wednesday entwined her fingers with his and hoped for the best.

She kissed the corner of his mouth. "I'm going to shock you."

He looked at her pretty face, admired the shape of her mouth, the slant of her eyes, the cute pertness of her nose, the wisps of molasses-colored hair draping across her cheeks. He couldn't think of anything that would change his mind about loving her.

"Were you married before? I can deal with that."

She shook her head. "Nothing like that."

"You hear voices?" He shrugged. "I can deal with that. My great aunt heard voices. No big deal. I just won't take you out very much." He smiled and slid his hand up her thigh. "Which is fine with me. I can think of lots to do in the privacy of our own bedroom."

Wednesday removed his hand from her leg and stood up.

"I wish it were only voices," she told him, her voice quiet.

"Spill it, so we can move on."

"I come from a different background than you."

"Is that all? Are you Catholic?"

"Tom," she placed a hand on his shoulder, "do you believe in magic?"

"Like Houdini?" He teased her again. He couldn't help it. She was so adorable and so incredibly serious. Right now he didn't want to be serious. He wanted to laugh with her and kiss her and love her. He kissed the back of her hand.

"Sort of. Except Houdini's hocus-pocus wasn't real. It was all illusion created for entertainment."

"What does this have to do with your secret? I already know you practice magic. I saw the broom and mop, remember?" He trailed kisses up her arm.

"I don't practice magic." She took a deep breath. "I am magic, Tom."

"What?" He stopped kissing her, raising his head to look into her pretty face.

She backed away from him. "I'm a witch."

Silence descended between them.

He stared at her in complete bewilderment. Then he started to laugh. Deep, resonating laughter. It filled the entire kitchen.

"Stop laughing. I'm not kidding."

"Wednesday, you have some sense of humor."

"I'm not joking. Honestly, I'm a witch. I can prove it to you."

"Well, you've bewitched me." He lunged for her. She ran away, out of his reach. He laughed so hard he could barely stand. He collapsed back into the chair.

"You don't believe me," she accused. "I wouldn't make up such a story."

"Come here, my little witch." He snatched her about the waist and hauled her into his lap.

She struggled in his arms. "I AM A WITCH."

He covered her lips with his.

"What will it take to make you believe me?"

"Try a little hocus-pocus," he suggested.

"If you insist."

She murmured something incoherent.

The clutter on the counter vanished. Plates, bowls, forks and spoons cleaned and neatly put away. And his battering mess evaporated, leaving a sparkling stovetop.

Tom looked about him with astonishment. "Okay, I think you're in the wrong profession. How did you manage such a feat? Nice trick. What's the secret?"

"You still don't believe I'm a witch."

"Don't be ridiculous."

She whispered something that sounded suspiciously like an incantation.

And the world whirled around them.

Chapter Thirteen

In a matter of seconds they stood in the middle of the backyard.

"Do you believe me now?"

He stared hard at Wednesday as if seeing her for the very first time.

"Where did the kitchen go?" he asked hoarsely.

"It never moved. We moved."

"You? You're a witch? The very idea is absurd. Witches don't exist. They're fairy tales, figments of some author's imagination, in the same category as vampires and werewolves." He rubbed his eyes, blinked a couple of times, and rubbed his eyes again in disbelief. "Not possible. This is not possible."

"Do you believe me?"

"This is not real. I must be dreaming."

Wednesday's heart ached. She knew what was coming. He'd run from her once the reality set in. His logical, scientific, mortal brain wouldn't be able to accept the fact she was a witch.

"It's real. It's my secret."

"Witches aren't real."

"They are. I come from a long line of witches, Tom. And you don't want to know how old I am."

He paled considerably. "How old are you?"

"Do you really want to know?"

He nodded.

She calculated quickly in her head. She forgot at times how old she really was. "I am one hundred and twenty years old but I resemble a mortal woman in her early thirties."

He fell backwards from the shock. A wicker

chair materialized, catching him in his fall. "I don't believe this." He closed his eyes and ran his fingers through his hair. "So, you are immortal."

"I have a lifespan. All witches do. We just live longer than humans, and we don't look our actual age."

"So, you will look as you do now in fifty years?" he inquired.

She winced, nodding.

"And when I'm eighty and ancient looking, you'll still look as beautiful and youthful as you do now."

Wednesday nodded again. "But I can drink a potion that makes me age with you. It's temporary."

"Temporary meaning my lifespan?"

"Yes."

He covered his face with shaking hands. "This is a cruel joke."

Wednesday's throat grew tight. She fought back hot tears. She would not cry. She had to be strong. She had expected this.

"It isn't a joke. I really am a witch."

Tom dropped his hands, resting palms upon his knees. "But you don't look like a witch."

Wednesday laughed. Even she could hear it was filled with the bitterness and loneliness, a disenchanted laugh. "You mean with green skin and warts and a horrid personality?"

"Yes."

"Halloween creates such horrible stereotypes about us. We aren't the only ones who have been misrepresented by the holiday. My cousin Harold, a werewolf, has filed grievances."

He stood. "Why are you doing this?" He demanded, frustration in his voice.

Her heart fell. "You don't want to believe."

"This is ridiculous."

"But how else do you explain the kitchen, being transported out here, and the lawn chair you were just sitting on."

"I must have not seen it," he said, glancing at the chair.

She crossed arms over her chest. "And the other two things?"

He was silent, falling back down into the chair.

"What about the tea party Jenna told you about?"

"What are you talking about?"

Wednesday snapped her fingers. Another chair appeared. She sat down in it, crossing her ankles in very lady-like fashion. Tom, looking quite shocked by the arrival of another chair out of thin air, leaned so far back in his chair, it toppled over.

Wednesday quickly righted the chair and Tom with a flick of her finger. "Tom, are you all right?"

"I'm fine," he muttered. He clutched the chair arms, his knuckles bright white.

"Remember the fictional characters at the tea party?"

His eyes grew huge. "Not possible," he whispered.

"They came to tea last week and played a game of crazy croquet with your daughters."

"You expect me to believe my girls played with characters from a book?"

"I don't expect you to believe anything" she sighed "but at least try to keep an open mind about these things."

"These things?" he asked. He shook his head from side to side. "These aren't normal things."

"No." Wednesday moved her chair closer to his. It floated up in the air, landing directly next to his. "I told you it was a big secret and that it would change everything. Have your feelings changed for me, Tom?"

"I don't know. You're not who I thought you were." He gulped. "You're telling me you are a magical creature with the ability to summon chairs and clean kitchens with a few words or a snap of your fingers. And you can bring storybook characters to life."

She nodded, her heart aching, every nerve on edge.

"An actual witch?"

"Yes," she whispered.

Fear consumed her. She had no idea what was going to happen. Losing Tom terrified her, she was glad to finally be able to confess her secret. A heavy weight lifted from her shoulders. Whatever happened now was out of her control. It was in his hands.

She reached out to him, her fingers brushing his. "It doesn't change the fact I love you."

He jerked his hand from hers. He didn't look upon her face. He glanced over her shoulder, toward the flower gardens and guesthouse.

Wednesday knew the type of thoughts going through his head. She didn't need to be a mind reader to see the betrayal he felt behind his expression. She reached for him, her fingers trembling as they brushed against his arm. He jerked away from her. His eyes narrowed. She saw distrust in the green pools.

"No, Tom. No."

"If you are who you say you are, then tell me, was this, the love I have for you, all a spell?"

The harshness of his voice shattered her heart. Tears cascaded down her cheeks. She reached out to him again. He pulled away. Anger made his cheeks red. The distaste in his eyes made her gasp.

"It wasn't. I didn't cast any spell on you. I promise."

He glared at her.

"Don't you believe me?" Her entire body started to tremble. "Oh, Tom, please trust me. I didn't put a love spell on you. I can't."

"You can't?" he snapped.

"There are codes we follow."

"Codes? Ethical codes?"

"Yes," she muttered, her voice barely a whisper, "but we can't mess with death or love or the ways of the heart. That is magic we can't even begin to control. It is more powerful than any spell we can cast."

"You put a spell on me to make me love you," he growled. "No one falls in love this quickly."

Wednesday winced at the fury vibrating in his voice. This was going worse than she imagined. It never dawned on her he'd come to the crazy conclusion she hexed him. But she couldn't really blame him. If she were in his shoes, she'd think the same thing.

Tom stood and kicked the chair. It rolled down the incline of the immaculate lawn, coming to a stop a few feet from Wednesday's front door. He paced in front of her, fast and furious strides. "I hired you to take care of my children." He groaned. His hands made fists at his sides.

"I'm qualified."

"How?" he asked.

"I'm a graduate of Magical Nanny University. And I'm an employee with the Magical Nannies Foundation for Children."

"Stop it. Just stop it. I don't want to hear any more."

"Tom, please, listen-"

"You go around messing with people's lives!" he accused, glaring at her.

"No. We try to help children and their families."

"How? By lying to them, by pretending to be someone you aren't?"

Wednesday sniffed. She swiped the tears from her cheeks, the salty drops now dropping in a steady flow. She couldn't stop crying.

"I never lied to you. I am a nanny."

"Just a nanny who happens to be a witch. You left that fact off your résumé."

"I'm sorry," Wednesday choked out. "I only wanted to help."

"You're a fraud."

Pain twisted her heart Her heart at the words. "You don't mean that."

"I do."

A sob tore from her throat. She bowed her head, letting the tears tumble to her lap, staining her flowered skirt with wet splotches.

"Tom, I didn't put a spell on you. I didn't. I wouldn't do such a dishonest thing," she sniffed miserably. "I wouldn't trick you or the girls into caring for me. You must believe me." She added in a whisper, "Trust your heart, Tom."

"I don't know what to believe or trust anymore." He turned his back on her. "Leave, please. I need time to think."

Wednesday refused to give up. She ran to him and threw her arms around him. "I love you. I do love you. Our love is the greatest magic of all."

"I just can't deal with this right now. I need time to decide if what I felt was real…if I really love you."

"You do. I know you do."

He turned to look at her. The tortured look in his eyes made her cry harder. She caused him such pain. She hated herself for it. He traced the lines of her face with one shaking finger.

"How can I know what I feel?" he asked.

"You have to trust me and your heart."

"No. Please go." He disentangled from her arms.

"Okay, I'll be gone by this afternoon." She reached for him one last time.

He shook his head. "No. Not right away. The children need you. You can't up and leave them.

They'll be devastated. They've grown so attached to you."

Tom was right. She couldn't abandon the children. Besides, they were her first priority, the reason she was here.

"And I need time to- "

"Find another nanny," she finished for him. "I'll stay as long as the children need me. I owe them that."

Wednesday spun on her heel and ran across the lawn, racing up the winding path through the flower gardens to the guest cottage. She slammed the front door behind her and slumped against it. Heart-wrenching sobs shook her body. She sunk to the floor.

She'd lost him. It was over.

It was worse than that.

He distrusted her, convinced an enchanted charm had ignited his love for her.

She spent the night sacked out on the couch watching an old movie. The tears refused to stop. So did the throbbing pain in her heart. She tried to vanish away her woes by eating two cartons of chocolate ice cream.

Inky and Jazz watched her with lazy curiosity. They took up residence at her feet, purring contentedly while she burst into uncontrollable sobs.

"This can't be the way it ends," she cried to them.

Inky yawned. Jazz flicked his tail.

"Isn't love supposed to conquer all?"

Jazz moved his ears. Inky licked his paw.

"How can I leave him? I can't do it. I just can't."

The cats remained silent, staring back at her through slanted eyes.

"You don't care if I'm sad or not. Your only concern is food. I'd love to have your uncomplicated life. Maybe I should turn myself into a cat."

Not that it made any difference. She'd still feel horrible even with ears and a tail and whiskers. Being a cat would not banish Tom from her heart.

"I hate being in love."

But that wasn't true. She'd loved being in love. Nothing was more beautiful. It was the breaking-up part she could do without.

Eventually she managed to pull herself from the couch and crashed into bed. She couldn't think about packing and leaving the place she now thought of as home. She wanted to avoid leaving for as long as possible, hoping to give Tom time to come to his senses.

She still held onto the hope he'd show up on her doorstep, confess his undying love, and ask her to be his bride. She'd lost count of how many times she glanced expectantly at the door.

But he didn't come the next day or the next or the next. And he did not speak to her when their paths crossed in the house.

He wouldn't come. The answer was obvious. He couldn't accept who she was.

The pain in his eyes haunted her.

On the afternoon of the fourth day following her confession, Wednesday decided it was best to start packing. She needed to leave as soon as she said her goodbyes to the children. Tom had found a new caretaker for the children. He was taking a sabbatical from work to spend time with them.

Wednesday was thrilled for the girls. They would be overjoyed at the prospect of spending so much time with their father.

But she was miserable.

She grabbed the stuffed Halloween cat Tom had won for her the night of the carnival and was about to toss it into her bag, but she couldn't let it go. She held it tight to her heart, remembering the beautiful night they shared together. Tears erupted. She pushed the stuffed cat into the ratty carpetbag and snapped it shut. She supposed the garbage was the best place for the stuffed toy, but she couldn't part with it. It connected her to Tom.

Wednesday glanced at her watch. It was three o'clock. She was supposed to go up to the house and see the girls at four.

She looked over at the door and sighed. Tom wasn't going to stop her from leaving.

Inky and Jazz rubbed against her ankles.

"Ready to go?" she asked.

The two cats sat on their haunches and yowled softly.

"Okay, but first I need to go and say goodbye to the girls. I'm not leaving without seeing them."

Wednesday walked across the small guesthouse and swung open the door.

And walked right into Tom's chest.

"Oh!" she cried, startled to find a solid wall of muscle standing on her front steps.

"Hi."

Her heart leapt. She stepped back and tilted her head back so she could see his handsome face. He looked relieved to see her.

"Hi."

He also looked nervous and slightly embarrassed. "Can I come in?" he asked.

Did she dare hope he came to stop her from leaving? Would her fantasy actually come true? Wednesday didn't know, but she was thrilled to see him. And he didn't seem angry with her any longer.

"Of course."

He stepped around her and walked inside.

Wednesday closed the door.

Tom spied her packed luggage. It seemed to startle him.

"I told you I was leaving today."

"I know. I don't know where to begin."

Wednesday gestured toward the sofa. "Do you want to sit down?"

Tom nodded. He was very fidgety. He sat down on the couch and pulled a piece of crumbled paper from his pocket. He held it out to her.

"I found this in Jenna's room last night after I stopped in to give her a kiss. It was tucked under a book on her nightstand."

Wednesday stared at the piece of paper, not sure what it was.

"It's her letter, her ad for a nanny, the very one you claimed to have received the first day we met."

Wednesday's fingers shook as she grasped the wrinkled paper. She sat down beside him and smoothed out the parchment against her knees. Her throat tightened as she read Jenna's simple, innocent words.

"I gave this back to her the night the girls interviewed me."

"That's what I figured, although somehow I missed that exchange."

Wednesday grimaced. "Another secret kept from you," she whispered. "I'm sorry."

"You told me about the ad. I refused to believe it, as I've done with everything else you've told me. It's me who needs to apologize. I've had to do that a lot lately."

She placed a gentle hand on his arm. "You don't have to, Tom. I completely understand."

"But I hurt you. I never wanted to do that."

She shrugged as if it didn't matter. But it did. His words and actions cut into her deeply.

"It was such a shock. I didn't know how to handle it."

"I know." She folded up the letter with tender fingers and offered it back to him.

"No. You keep it. It's meant for you.

She would treasure it always. "Thank you."

"I've been a fool. I can't believe I accused you of enchanting me, of using magic to make me care for you. I shouldn't have done that." He brushed his fingers across the back of her hand. "You did enchant me, but I know it had nothing to do with magic."

Wednesday watched his fingers curl about hers. She dared not allow herself to hope. She didn't know if she could survive her heart being demolished again.

"I think our love is magic. It isn't my hocus-pocus. It is a mortal magic, which makes it all the more wonderful. It is real," she whispered.

"You still love me after all I said and did?"

"Of course I do. Love doesn't go away because of a disagreement."

"We had a little more than an argument," he chuckled.

"I wanted you to know the truth. I never meant to keep anything from you or to cause you pain."

"I've been thinking about what happened. I treated you horribly. I had no right."

"You had every right."

"Don't leave. Witch or not you've been a great influence on my girls," he said, "and on me."

Wednesday gasped when she saw the love shining in his eyes. "You love me despite everything?"

Tom snaked an arm about her waist. "I'd be a fool to not recognize true love and grab onto it and hold it tight."

The intensity of his eyes mesmerized her. Ireland couldn't be greener.

"Oh, Tom, I feel the same way."

"Then you'll stay?"

"I'm supposed to leave. I've been placed in a different home. I have another job to go to."

"I can't let you leave." His arm tenderly

tightened around her slim waist. "I love you. I admit I was foolish and irrational before, but now I know what I want. I want you and I don't give a damn if you're the most powerful witch out there. You aren't, are you?"

Wednesday laughed at his nervous sidelong glance. "I'm still sort of in the apprentice stage."

He grinned. "I promise I won't turn into a Darrin Stephens. You can practice magic if you want to."

She returned his grin. "I have a feeling I won't need to."

"You don't have any crazy relatives who'll be popping by?"

Wednesday arched an eyebrow. "I do."

"How many?" He looked so horrified she felt sorry for him.

"You don't want to know."

"Well, Tuesday seems normal."

"Oh, she is probably the most normal."

He gulped and took a deep breath. "I don't care. I want you in my life, but I'll need some time with that. You don't think they'll turn me into rabbits or anything?"

"I won't let them," Wednesday promised. She looped her arms over his shoulders. "Tell me again."

"Tell you what?" His smile deepened.

"You know."

Tom lifted her onto his lap. "I love you, Wednesday Green."

Wednesday's heart danced. "There is one more thing I should tell you."

Tom kissed the tip of her nose. "And what is that?"

"My name isn't Wednesday Green."

He groaned. "Dare I ask what it really is? I sort of liked your name."

"Wednesday is my first name," she said softly,

"but I don't have a last name."

He kissed one of her dimples. "Oh?"

"Witches don't have last names."

"Go on."

"I picked Green because it was the color of your eyes."

The corners of his eyes crinkled with amusement. "That's very romantic."

"You think so?"

His answer was a kiss.

Wednesday sighed blissfully in his arms.

"So, you don't have a last name?"

She shook her head.

Tom bounded off the couch with her still in his arms.

"What are you doing?"

"I want to show you something."

He carried her out into the summer sunshine.

"Where are we going?"

"You'll see."

Wednesday clung to him as he walked across the lawn. She giggled every time he stopped to cover her lips with his.

"Tell me."

"Don't you enjoy surprises?" he asked.

"Of course I do."

"If I tell you then it won't be a surprise."

She laid her head on his shoulder and closed her eyes. "You love me even though I'm not mortal."

His lips grazed her temple. "I told you I didn't care about that. I only care about you. Now keep those eyes closed."

Her eyelids fluttered open.

"Keep them shut."

She obeyed him, nuzzling closer.

A few seconds later he whispered in her ear, "You can open your eyes now."

Wednesday opened her eyes and gasped in

surprise.

Sunflowers filled his entire bedroom.

She kissed his cheek. "You remembered."

"Look again."

She did. Candlelight illuminated the room. It took her breath away.

"Thank you."

"I think you missed the most important thing."

"I don't need anything more than the flowers and the candles."

"But I went through a lot of work to pick it out."

Wednesday's heart stopped.

"Pick what out?"

"Look." He pointed to the middle of his huge bed.

Wednesday's vision blurred. A glittering, shimmering diamond ring winked back at her, nestled in a blue velvet box.

"I thought," her voice caught, "you were so angry with me. I thought that was why you stayed away."

Tom set her on her feet.

His fingers splayed tenderly against her back. "I was upset but I got over it fast. The moment you ran away, I knew nothing mattered except how much I loved you."

Wednesday started to cry. "It seems I have an endless supply of tears today."

His lips brushed the top of her head. "There's a card next to the box."

Wednesday knelt onto the bed. She picked up the oversized card, her eyes lingering on the sparkling engagement ring. The card was from the girls.

"What does it say?"

"Don't you know?" she asked.

He shook his head. "Tell me."

"They say they love me," she drew a shaky breath, "and ask if I will be their new mommy."

"Will you?" Tom lifted the velvet box and got

down on one knee. "Will you be their new mommy? Will you be my wife? I can give you the last name you've been without."

She smiled through her tears. "Yes, I'll marry you."

Tom slipped the ring from the velvet box. His fingers shook as he placed it on her finger. She spread her fingers wide so she could enjoy the ring. It was gorgeous, a square-cut diamond in a silver band. It caught the light from the candles and shimmered brilliantly.

"I'm going to be Wednesday Anderson. Mrs. Tom Anderson."

Tom drew her close. "I can't wait to make you my wife. I love you."

"I love you."

His tender kiss turned passionate. Soon they were draped across the bed, hands searching frantically, pieces of clothing falling away.

Wednesday panicked. "Wait. Where are the girls?"

He smiled that adorable crooked smile. "With Mom."

"You've thought of everything."

He removed one of her shoes and caressed her leg. "Of course. I didn't want anything to ruin this perfect moment."

"And nothing will," she sighed.

"We're getting married as soon as possible."

"Halloween is right around the corner. What do you think?" she asked.

"By Halloween? Two months?" His eyes twinkled. "I'm sure you can arrange it."

She threw back her head and laughed. Her hair fanned out across the pillow. "I think I can whip up a wedding in two months."

"I thought you might be able to, my little witch," he whispered against her collarbone.

No spell could make her feel the way Tom did.

She surrendered to his embrace and to the delicious mortal magic conjured up by two people in love, a magic as old as time.

Epilogue

Eighteen months later…

Lumina couldn't believe how things had turned out. It seemed as though so much time had passed since little Jenna wrote the ad for her perfect nanny. She'd been so sad when her father had hardly ever been home.

Then Lumina arranged for Wednesday to arrive in Jenna's life, in Tom's life, and she was just what the Anderson family had needed.

Lumina beamed with pride as she watched the happy family from her perch on the fireplace mantle. She'd played a small part in the match, even if she'd advised Wednesday against it. The odds were against them, a witch and a mortal, but they seemed to be making it work.

There was no doubt Tom Anderson loved Wednesday, and Wednesday loved him with her whole heart. Now, they were husband and wife.

Lumina had enjoyed the wedding, hiding in Wednesday's bridal bouquet. It had been a lovely wedding, so filled with love and happiness and hope, just as any wedding should be.

Jenna, Tamra and Michaela had been flower girls. Wednesday had looked just like a princess, her dress long, white cascading silk. She'd worn a tiara on her head. Lumina smiled as remembered how it sparkled in the summer sunlight.

Wednesday was no longer a nanny. She was a loving mother of four. They'd welcomed another bundle of joy nine months ago.

Lumina glanced over at Tom and Wednesday curled up on the couch together. His arm draped across her shoulders. Her hands rested on his leg. They talked quietly and smiled as only two people in love do. Tom always smiled now. He was so happy.

Lumina fluttered silently out of the living room and flew up the stairs and down the upstairs hallway. Soft cooing came from one of the rooms. She paused in front of a closed door for a moment before pushing it open.

The cooing stopped.

Lumina moved towards the crib.

And looked right into the brown eyes of Wednesday's baby girl.

The nine-month-old giggled upon spying the little fairy. Her eyes glowed. She smiled. Two teeth gleamed bright at her sister.

"Hi, Cora," Lumina whispered. She sat down on the crib rail, gazing down at the beautiful child. She looked like Wednesday except she had her father's brilliant green eyes.

Baby Cora laughed and clapped her chubby hands. She started speaking in her baby tongue.

"Yes, you do have a lovely family," Lumina responded to the little girl's chatter. Fairies understood the language of babies. "You are a very lucky little girl."

Cora giggled and grabbed at her toes. Lumina smiled. She was so adorable with her riot of dark curls framing her round face. She was the happiest of babies. She had no reason not to be happy. She was so loved.

"How are you today, Cora?" Lumina asked softly. She wiggled her fingers at Wednesday's child.

Cora grabbed Jenna's fingers. "I'm great," she blabbered.

"Whatcha doing?"

Lumina turned.

Jenna stood in the doorway with Tamra and Michaela. They knew all about Lumina. Since Lumina was Cora's godmother, Wednesday had thought it best to introduce her to the children.

"I'm talking to Cora."

"She's napping."

"She isn't. Look."

Jenna and Tamra traipsed in, Michaela at their heels.

The three stared at their cooing, laughing sister as she blabbered.

"I can't understand her," complained Tamra. "When will she talk like us?"

Jenna shrugged. "Someday."

"Soon enough, children. Don't rush her. She'll grow up faster than you realize."

Cora grasped the bars of the crib with tiny hands, and pulled herself up. She crowed with triumphant when she at last stood up straight.

"I hope she likes tea parties," Tamra said.

"She will," Lumina assured.

Cora smiled again, revealing dimples in her cheeks.

"I hope she likes us." Tamra kissed one of Cora's chubby legs.

"She will. She already does. And your job is to watch over her."

Cora bounced up and down. The crib started to shake. She giggled. "Sisters!" she exclaimed in the language only Lumina could understand. It was baby gibberish to the three girls watching her with adoration on their faces.

Lumina's heart swelled with love. She was so happy Wednesday had made her part of the family by asking her to be godmother.

"And what are you four doing in here?"

Lumina and the girls spun around.

Wednesday stood at the door with Tom right

behind her. Both smiled warmly.

"I just wanted to see Cora." Jenna felt guilty for interrupting Cora's nap. "She wasn't sleeping. She was wide-awake. Honest. Lumina was here first."

Wednesday walked across the room. She kissed all three girls on the cheek and grinned at Lumina.

She lifted Cora and cradled her close. She looked up at Lumina. "Isn't she perfect, Lumina?"

Lumina nodded. "As perfect as a mortal baby can be."

"She's half witch. Don't forget that," said Wednesday. She turned her gaze onto her precious child. "Look at you. Not tired at all." Wednesday cuddled Cora, brushing her lips across the baby's soft black curls. "You should be sleeping."

Cora blinked and tried to pull at one of Wednesday's long tendrils of hair.

"Don't you dare," Wednesday scolded. She grabbed one flailing fist and kissed it lovingly. "I've lost enough hair thanks to you."

Lumina smiled at Wednesday. She grinned back.

"Come on, girls. How about we play a game?"

Tamra and Michaela bounded over to Tom, agreeing enthusiastically to his suggestion.

"With the Wonderland characters?" Michaela asked.

Tom's laughter warmed Lumina's heart. He was a different man.

"I guess," he said, giving his youngest daughter a gentle hug. "We'll have to wait for your mom. Ready, dear?"

Lumina didn't miss the loving glance Tom shared with Wednesday. She was thrilled her dearest friend had found someone to share her life with. It was proof happy endings still existed.

"We'll be there in a moment," Wednesday said.

"Don't be too long." He left the room, Tamra and

Michaela following close at his heels.

"So, what do you think of your little sister?" Wednesday asked Jenna.

"I like her a lot."

"I'm very glad you do. I like her too."

Cora burst into spontaneous laughter. Jenna joined in and Wednesday did, too.

Lumina couldn't resist the laughter and started giggling as well. Her laughter sounded like tiny chimes.

Wednesday smiled, winking at Lumina. She took Jenna's hand in hers.

"And Cora adores her big sister," Wednesday said.

"Can we read her a book?" Jenna asked, looking quite pleased with herself.

"Of course we can. You pick one out."

Jenna walked over to a nearby bookcase and selected a nursery rhyme book.

"Good choice." They sat down at the window seat. Lumina fluttered off the crib rail and joined them, sitting on Wednesday's shoulder.

Jenna snuggled close to Wednesday. "You smell good."

Wednesday hugged her with one arm. "Thanks." She opened the book and began to read.

Lumina enjoyed listening to Wednesday read. She had a lovely voice, a voice sounding like music.

Cora tried to grab at the pages of the book. She pointed and giggled and cooed and wiggled her toes.

"You like stories, don't you?" Wednesday gave Cora's nose a kiss.

"I think her favorite is the one about Jack and Jill," said Jenna.

Cora scrunched up her face. "It is not," she squealed in her baby tongue.

Lumina hid a smile behind her hand.

Jenna and Wednesday were oblivious. Jenna's

head rested against Wednesday's shoulder. Wednesday read a few more rhymes before closing the book and putting Cora back in her crib.

Cora's eyes fluttered closed, her long lashes swept across her rounded cheeks.

Jenna kissed one of Cora's hands.

"Come on," Wednesday whispered.

Jenna took her outstretched hand. Lumina rode on Wednesday's shoulder.

"Are you joining us for the croquet match, Lumina?"

"Wouldn't miss it."

"So, do you think we'll beat the Mad Hatter today?" Wednesday asked Jenna, closing the door behind them.

Jenna shook her head. "He always wins."

Wednesday ruffled her hair affectionately as they walked down the hallway.

Lumina heard something odd coming from Cora's bedroom. "Do you hear that?"

Jenna stopped and cocked her head to one side. "What's that noise?"

Wednesday paused to listen. "It sounds like sheep. What in the world?" She spun on her heel and ran back to the nursery.

Jenna raced after her.

The sound grew louder.

Wednesday pushed open the door. "Oh, my goodness!"

"I guess, now we all know which is her favorite nursery rhyme," said Lumina softly.

Sheep filled the entire nursery. The fluffy white creatures were ba-ba-baaing. They seemed quite confused. And in the middle of the sheep stood Little Bo Peep, looking rather displaced in a baby's nursery and not out in the field looking for her lost sheep.

Cora squealed with laughter. She stood in her

crib, bouncing up and down, pride in her beaming smile.

"She did this?" Jenna asked, her eyes round as saucers.

Wednesday nodded.

"Looks like your daughter takes after you," whispered Lumina.

"Don't I know it," Wednesday whispered back as she swept her arm through the air. The sheep and Miss Little Bo Peep vanished back into the book.

Wednesday looked at Jenna. "Let me tell Daddy about your sister's magical powers, okay?" She took Jenna's hand, leading her from the room, and shutting the door behind them.

"Okay," Jenna agreed.

"I don't think your father's ready to find out his daughter has inherited anymore of my unique characteristics. He may faint from the shock."

Lumina shook her head. "He should have suspected it was a possibility."

"Yes, but *a possibility* is easier to accept than reality."

Wednesday hugged Jenna tight and kissed her on the cheek. "Go on, find your sisters. It's a beautiful day to play outside."

Jenna slipped from her arms and ran off, disappearing around the corner. Lumina heard her clambering down the stairs and shouting for her father.

Wednesday groaned.

"My guess is you better tell him now. Little girls don't know how to keep secrets." Lumina lifted off Wednesday's shoulder.

"I suppose you're right about that." Wednesday kissed the top of Cora's head.

Tom's booming voice filled the house. "Wednesday, I need to talk with you for a moment."

Lumina giggled at Wednesday's panicked look.

"I think he knows."

"Sounds that way. Guess I better go calm him down."

"Your life will never be boring."

Wednesday looked at Lumina. Her eyes sparkled. "Definitely not. It will always be interesting. Thanks, Lumina. Thanks for my amazing life."

Lumina kissed her cheek. "Thank yourself, darling. You owe your happiness to yourself, to you and Tom. I only brought you here."

"Oh, you had a little more to do with all this than just that."

Lumina blushed.

"You knew, didn't you?"

"Knew what, Wednesday?" Lumina asked, feigning innocence.

"That something connected Tom and me."

Lumina fluttered close to Wednesday's face. "I'll never admit to doing anything. You and Tom fell in love all on your own. You didn't need my help for that. I just took a few obstacles out of your way."

"It still helped."

Lumina kissed the tip of Wednesday's nose.

Footsteps sounded on the stairs.

Wednesday smiled nervously. "Wish me luck." She waved as she jogged down the hallway, her hair trailed out behind her, the scent of lilac and lavender floated around Lumina.

"You won't need it, darling," murmured Lumina. "He loves you. You're a lucky girl."

Lumina slipped out the hallway window and flew in the direction of the sunset.

Someone else needed her help.

About the Author

Amy Hahn has been a writer for as long as she can remember. Notebooks filled with her creative stories were a constant companion throughout childhood, high school and college years.

She has a bachelor's and master's degree in journalism and has worked as an editor and writer for various magazines and for online news web sites. She has also worked as a television news producer, college instructor, and writes patient education material for one of the world's top medical organizations.

Her first love has always been romance writing, especially historical and paranormal. She lives in Minnesota with her husband Chris. Her hobbies include reading, family genealogy, horseback riding, and probably too much television and movie viewing.

Thank you for purchasing
this Wild Rose Press publication.
For other wonderful stories of romance,
please visit our on-line bookstore at
www.thewildrosepress.com.

For questions or more information
contact us at
info@thewildrosepress.com.

The Wild Rose Press
www.TheWildRosePress.com